AuthorHouse™ UK Ltd.
500 Avebury Boulevard
Central Milton Keynes, MK9 2BE
www.authorhouse.co.uk
Phone: 08001974150

First published by AuthorHouse 4/3/2008

ISBN: 978-1-4343-2453-5 (sc)

Printed in the United States of America
Bloomington, Indiana

This book is printed on acid-free paper.

Prologue:

Maria, a beautiful girl in her late teens has finally found the love and security that her adopted family are able to give her. Her early childhood had been riddled with untold misery and suffering, which continued well into puberty. But now, three years of happiness has secured a meaningful relationship with life, turning a once introverted personality into that of an astute and dependable member of a society she could accept.

Her future looked promising, but life could be cruel! Oh yes, very cruel indeed. And such symptomatic reversals in a life unaffected by greed or suffering would eventually affect the whole family too include Maria, inflicting unimaginable horror that would leave a confused Detective Chief Inspector Lawson trying desperately to grapple with each situation as it arose.

A story where sexual orientation blends easily as a contrivance instilling the means to an end, and were human suffering connives with evil, though at the same time offering intrigue, suspense and evaluation to the reader as too who or what is the killer. Read on and enjoy!

The Author:

The House That Jack Built!

Mrs Amy Martins sat pensive and troubled, her worries extending to the dubious relationship her daughter had embarked on with Tom Harper, a young man whom she had always considered as wayward and untrustworthy, though that certainly hadn't been the case with Maria. Maria's feelings retained those of a girl in her late teens whose infatuation had developed into a strong and developed relationship, though love was certainly not on the agenda. She was far too young and intelligent, and she knew it!

"That sort of stuff can all wait until I've established a career for myself," Maria exclaimed reassuringly to her concerned mother, casually stroking the long strands of dark-brown hair with a deep affection as she attempted to convince her that Tom was not all that he'd been made out to be by those who had taken an obvious dislike to him.

"Anyhow, what did it matter if he had left home at sixteen to live with his grand-dad? After all, his parents had been detestable to him and had always considered him a far lesser mortal than his darling brother George," she motioned, pausing for breath just for a moment. "And anyway, George is twenty-four and three years older, and a bullying bastard," Maria venomously suggested to an astonished mother, who went on to denounce such accusations being made against the Harpers but thought better of it, though remained quick to point out her disapproval at such a display of anger.

"After all, Fred and Sue Harper were certainly no friends of hers," she mused with a degree of scorn and indignation, "and especially after that letter they'd sent complaining about the smoke from the burning rubbish. Why, it had after all been well past 6pm, and the wind was blowing the opposite way from her damn washing, and they lived more than two streets away, and if she thought that she was going to pay for her ruined dress she could bloody well take a running jump," she muttered reflectively, her mind now filled with more 'ands' than she could possibly digest, though still they continued to haunt her. "And, as for her bra and knickers, why, they were already dirty when she hung the things up, obviously the wrong soap powder!" she smirked to herself, knowing only too well that the cause had most probably been the smoke. "Still, shame!" she smiled secretively, having now fully exhausted her contempt of Sue Harper.

Leaving her mother to her ponderings Maria dutifully removed herself from the room, deciding that perhaps the best cause of action would be not to mention Tom, and, not to bring him over. Just for the moment! She had always had the good fortune or otherwise to have a string of boyfriends following her for her attentions - and more if they were lucky - but now she had found Tom, a good looking lad with dark curly hair, a laughing smile, and a build that only a girl could dream of, she remained determined not to let him go! Not that she had any worries on that score. He adored her!

Making her way up a narrow flight of wooden steps that resisted her every move with a resounding creak, she arrived at the first floor of the listed Grade 11 thatched mill-cottage - a mill-cottage that her parents had always dreamt of calling their own, having worked hard to secure such a dream - she entered her bedroom. Making her way to the shallow, leaded-light widows, she threw them open with a feeling of exhilaration as she took a deep and devouring breath of the sweet smelling air. The scented fragrance of a variety of flowers and shrubs from the garden below shrouded her in an enthusiastic display of satisfaction to one who appreciated their splendour, offering themselves as messengers from nature's eternal endeavours to pander to the enlightenment that the human spirit sought to reap from its botanical entrapment.

⚶⚶

The fields and woodlands beyond only served as a reminder that out there lay a feast to be savoured, a feast full of wonderments as the birds sang in an almost harmonious defiance to the human noises that offered little more than annoying decibels, with the hum of the honeybee dutifully going about its business blending discreetly with that of dragonflies and a multitude of brightly coloured butterflies keen not to discriminate against those less fortunate insects that had little in the way of colour, or anything else for that matter.

"Summer in the beautiful county of Devon is one to be savoured," Maria sighed, as staring to the horizon she followed its undulating contours, yellow with the sway of golden corn and sun-kissed blossoms, stretching the imagination in a display of uniformed continuity on and on to disappear beyond the distant horizon, as if to remind those sceptics to its beauty that the best was still to come- Autumn! Maria sighed as once again she treasured such delights, realising how lucky she was to live in such delightful surrounds, and, in such a delightful village. The village of Tanstoll!

Sprawling casually across her bed she flipped over the pages of a magazine offering the occasional theoretical response to a quiz or puzzle that continued to annoy her.

" Why must I always get the dam thing wrong?" she announced to a spider that had unwittingly found itself crawling about on the second page, a second page that could soon see its demise as moving speedily away it just managed to escape with its life as the page was turned.

Article after article encouraged her in her duty to fulfil every girls dream. Serving to remind her that a good sexual appetite heartened the soul and, that if a condom was used at all times then she should enjoy the thrills and pleasures that heterosexual encounters could offer - though lesbian relationships also had their place in a society that had derived benefit in every fashionable deviation drawn to its fold - the following paragraph was quick to assure, causing Maria to scoff at such claims having experienced both in her young life.

At seventeen going on twenty-five Maria had a level head on shoulders that still bore the weight of hardship no young person should ever have had to endure. For a moment her mind dwelt back to her early childhood as she encountered an article on child abuse, reminding her of the endless stream of foster parents she had endured, nearly always ending up in heartbreak with some offering more though increasing her determination and resilience that one day she would have 'real parents'.

"Just like all her friends and classmates," she had insisted to herself tearfully, but now thankful of her own adopted family. Her mother had died in childbirth, and her father - a drunken lout who had abused her both mentally and physically - had been killed in a brawl outside the local pub. With no brothers or sisters and little other family that she was aware of - apart from an aging aunt she had distant memories of - she had ended up at the age of nine alone and vulnerable, though a great deal better off than she'd been with her father. Or so she thought!

Social services had intervened, taking her into care where her life had been a misery. Endless subjections to sexual harassment and bullying by older girls, whose jealousy of such an attractive girl - and one that at just eleven had offered early puberty having blessed her or otherwise with an almost fully developed figure - had encouraged their insistence to secure a taste of such highly evolved innocence. She had been left embarrassed and confused as to why she should have breasts and pubic hairs whilst none of the other girls her own age had reached anything like that stage. Revulsion had set in, with hate and despair mixing her emotions, convinced that all girls were the same and seeking solace in the friendly and eagerly reassuring confidence of one of the male supervisors.

A bad move!" she reflected angrily. He had used and abused, threatening her with anything and everything if she dare so breathe a word to, anyone! She hadn't, as he'd subjected her to an endless list of sexual deviations that even her father would have frowned on, taking her into her early teens traumatised, dejected and suicidal, and having now attained the opportunity of an early escape from these continuing nightmares.

Maria threw down the magazine in disgust, her memories confounding the reality of the present as she stared quietly at a bottle of Aspirin serving defiantly as a reminder to her despair, sitting on her bedside drawer in a defused acknowledgement to the past. Tears quickly developing from eyes clouded in the disparity of a life that she'd tried desperately to forget, and one she'd endeavoured to put behind her though with little success.

"A life that had been worse than hell," she reminded herself with conviction, the tears now streaming down cheeks now use to such intrusion. Her suicide bid had been a disaster, leaving her mind in turmoil her body physically drained as the chemicals had played havoc with her brain.

Slowly but surely she'd recovered in a hospital for the mentally ill - and one that determined that in no way would her stay be prolonged - with the doctors and psychiatrists convinced that she'd remain both physically scarred and mentally discordant for life. On both counts she proved them to be wrong, securing a complete recovery though refusing adamantly to return to "that stinking place" as she'd so eloquently named the 'Social services Home' that had been a curse sent from the depths of Hell.

At the age of just thirteen she would experience her first foster parents, and from there her life would have its ups and downs, bringing experiences in life that would offer her the ability to cope with a future that would remain insecure and wanting.

The word "dinner" echoed vibrantly up the staircase, to enlighten the world that yet another of Amy's specialities had been prepared. The family congregated around the enormous solid oak dinning-room table in an enthusiastic response to her call, leaving Maria to trip over the family cat in her endeavours not to be last once again. She was! Seating herself next to her mother she looked adoringly at her adopted family.

"I do love you dad," she announced to a startled Arthur, a dad that sat dutifully at the head of the table in an old fashioned family gathering that offered conversation and a feeling of 'belonging' to them all - and especially Maria - who although younger than her two brothers and sister could meet them equally on almost everything.

"And I love you," her father replied, flattered at such an instinctive remark, and never one to rebuke a note of affection from a family member.

Sonya - or Sonny as she'd been nicknamed by her family and closest friends - at almost twenty adored her younger sister, delighting in expanding on all things that were romantic in life, never failing to recount her multitude of failings and conquests in a life consumed with male adoration. Her dark eyes and alluring smile, together with a figure that was full and exuberating passion, remained the envy of the village girls, draining any resistance offered by those unassuming young men whose one desire it was to experience first hand those attributes that Sonny displayed with little modesty, melting to her demands like butter on a hot summers evening.

Her sexual appetite often had Maria gasping, delighting in hearing first hand of yet another intimate moment and something that she wished she too could find it in her heart to experiment with. But! Those horrendous memories of her childhood just wouldn't leave her alone.

"She would wait! Perhaps Tom would bring her out of herself, offer her the chance to taste a complete romantic and loving relationship on her terms, with an understanding of the traumas and torments she had suffered," she acknowledges soulfully, remaining convinced of his affections but unsure of his intentions. "But first! First, she would have to explain to him of her reservations and fears. And! Would he be sympathetic? If he loved her as he said then he would, if not, well!"

At twenty-three David was the eldest. He cared for her as he thought a brother should though often confusing it for something else, protecting her and ensuring that no boy would upset or harm her. She had often considered this a form of over-protectionism, verging on an obsession to shelter her from any indulgences that he might consider unworthy of her, although he would insist on showering her with gifts and on occasions appear to treat her with what might be considered as just a little bit more than that of a deep, 'brother/sister affiliation'. Without a steady girlfriend at times she had often wondered at his intentions, though to her he was just her brother and no more.

Peter on the other hand was adorable, and at twenty-one was going steady, though with little thought to his own relationship he would often insist that Maria 'tag along' and, that they should make up a 'threesome', much to the consternation of his long suffering girlfriend.

"Until she found the right one!" he had often said to Maria with a wink, wishing desperately that she would.

"Well! She had, and although her mother might disapprove her father, Sonny and Peter certainly didn't," Maria had decided venomously. David although remained strongly opposed, insisting that Tom was nothing but a layabout and far too old for her. He was of course jealous, though that was something he would never admit too! He saw Tom as some form of competing gladiator, ready to coerce his beloved sister away from the safety and security of her family and a brother who worshiped her, rebuking any suggestion that they were made for each other and continued unrelenting in lavishing Maria with gifts whilst sarcastically extending derogatory remarks in Tom's favour. She admonished his persistence whole-heartedly, though his resolute determination to induce a favourable reaction continued undeterred.

Her father was as likable and as lovable as her mother. "A girl he could feel proud to call his daughter," he would often suggest to Maria, leaving Amy having to remind him that he should feel proud of both daughters. Which of course he was! His strong arms exemplified his trade as the village blacksmith, a dying occupation but one passed down through generations and one he could feel proud of, especially since acquiring the franchise for the whole area.

Wealth had not passed them by, with wise investments on a buoyant stock market ensuring complete security and a substantial increase in the family coffers, allowing the opportunity for a good education – not only for the children – but an opportunity of further education for their parents.

"A wise head circulates a wiser understanding of life," their father would always say, and it proved true!

The purchase of 'Millrise' cottage proved a sensible investment as well as a marvellous place to live, a building seeping within a history of intrigue and suspense fuelled by the exaggerated minds of the locals. Its construction had taken place during the latter part of the eighteenth century and built to the specifications of a Mr Jack Salter, whose notoriety as a fraudster and unscrupulous land- owner did little to convince the village community that he meant well.

Talk of wrongful doings, of insidious and sinister innovations had been discussed, considered and accepted by villagers over many generations, and it was now an established fact amongst the village gossipers that at the time of excavation to secure the deep foundations required for such an ambitious venture, a young village-girl by the name of Rosy had slipped and fallen into the deep pit after loosing her way in the dark.

Unhurt, but finding herself unable to escape from her muddy and imprisoned confounds she had spent the night freezing, weak and terrified, her faint cries for help having gone unheeded. The cold had disorientated her, had instilled a sense of hopeless devolvement to a world that fantasised her mind in an illusion of spiritual awareness to her invincibility as she slept, and slept, and slept. It was the day following and still she slept, a sleep that now proved terminal with the icy conditions metamorphosing her body as slowly her mortal being departed from a world she once knew. Inadvertently she had been buried alive by the workmen, who'd received strict orders from their boss to fill the hole and to complete the foundations within the day or face the sack.

Her spirit had never settled, had tantalised and scared, her mournful cries lost in the wind, crying, calling for help in the night, though heard only by those whose intoxicated state would render them incapable in distinguishing the hoot from some unsuspecting owl to that of the call of the Ban chi. Or so it was said!

And so the story continued, with suggestions and exaggerations ranging from that of a succession of events considered as rather unfortunate - though all the same proving enough to blight the mill over many years - to a number of unexplained and horrifying deaths that could not be ignored. Deaths that although had been deemed as accidental, had never the less instigated a feeling of worry and fear, a fear deeply instilled within minds of simple peasant folk and strong enough to cause a widely felt belief that, "yes indeed the place must be haunted."

Jack Salter's mysterious death shortly after the mill's completion had never been fully justified, although it was certain that no tears were shed at his sudden departure from this world, on the contrary, there had been jubilant celebrations by those unfortunates that had experienced first hand the misery and pain he had incurred.

'Millrise' cottage had engaged in a notable list of extravagancies within its three acres of garden and scrub, offering the ideal setting for three ponies, a small number of goats and a few chickens that engaged from time to time in a torrid love affair courtesy of a proud, swaggering cockerel that strutted about in acknowledgement to its position and duty in life. Integrated within this domestic bliss a menagerie of birds and wildlife had taken up residence for the season, and with an abundance of fruit trees growing alongside an area designated to vegetables and the like the land had grown rich, offering a succulent display of lush greens that flourished in the fertile red Devonshire soil.

This relatively small patch of land had soon become self sufficient, and had continued to secure a never ending flow of fresh vegetables, with plenty left over for "the natives" as the locals had been so aptly named, though secret only to a family whose position in the village was still maturing.

The inclusion of a small swimming pool had not gone un-noticed by the neighbours, although any reference to jealousy had soon been overcome with invites to barbecues and the occasional midnight Soiree by the pool, dispelling at a stroke any fears that they may have had that feeling of, "not getting along with the neighbours". On the contrary, their popularity had expanded over the years, with inclusions for everyone in just about everything that was fundamentally part of the village social, academic and cultural life, offering them a multitude of rolls in a thriving business venture for a level of self support in an enterprising village community.

"Their little market garden would go a long way!" remarked an enthusiastic Amy. And it would!

The name 'Millrise' had taken it's name from the obvious, a converted mill come cottage complete with wheel and stream, standing on a small gradient offering excellent flow for a stream that still served the community. The exterior retained its old world charm, having incorporated all the original features - although the mill itself wasn't active - with the interior lavished in a mixture of both contemporary furnishings alongside that of revitalised timbered ceilings, and a gorgeous inglenook with each offering a degree of opulence that often embarrassed them in front of friends.

"No they weren't showing off," and, "yes they relished in its surrounds," remained the usual response to any slants or insinuations, though quick to emphasise, "that it hadn't been without hard work that had achieved such splendour. Money had certainly helped, but the spoils of their labour had offered more", they would quickly remind those who showed the slightest hint of jealousy, hinting, "that if they too got of their backsides, then of course they could do equally as well." Simple advice was also offered in the process, with emphasis laid on how to inaugurate such a venture. Something that understandably didn't always go down too well!

"Enterprise was the master and work the slave," insisted their father as he helped Maria side the table, his good nature transmuting the atmosphere from one of a melodramatic lack of enthusiasm to a consummation of mutual laughter as they entered into their individual pursuits for the evening. Sonny would help her mother in the kitchen and then prepare her notes for a university course -work that was now long overdue.

"But would be completed in good time," she insisted to her concerned mother. "Andy would understand if she didn't see him tonight," she muttered unconvincingly to herself, knowing only too well that Andy had been looking forward to something 'a little bit special' that evening, and something that she had to admit she had been looking forward too herself.

He was a hunk of a lad, with exceptional charm and wit and, he was rich. She smiled at what might have been as she rang him on her mobile, insisting that her exams were just a week away and that her finals followed two months on.

"Your sexual stimulate could surely wait until tomorrow," she crooned seductively to a poor Andy, who had spent the best part of a day preparing his flat to entertain this delightful creature in a lavish entrapment of erotica and consummation to a perfect evening, though his skills in the kitchen would have undoubtedly entailed digressing from a beautifully prepared home cooked dish to that of ordering a Chinese takeaway.

"Still, food and sex contradict each other," he had unconvincingly tried to assure her during their evenings spent together in a bedroom spilling over with every conceivable romantic innovation a girl could wish for.

"And I was so desperately looking forward to tomorrow evening," she sighed, unhappy at the thought of having to work tonight, though tingling in anticipation of what might be on offer as she whispered, "Goodnight sweet!" to a disappointed Andy.

Maria offered to sit with her sister, but was reminded by Sonny that Tom was due to meet her at the 'Travellers Arms' at nine, and with a fifteen minute taxi journey she would be late. "That's if you don't move now honey!" Sonny encouraged her with a concerned smile.

Returning to her bedroom Maria prepared to change, though not before glancing at the wall mirror for a moment as she studied herself from all angles. At five foot eight she retained an elegance that complimented a figure cloaked in sensual appraisal, offering more that just that of a very attractive girl. Lithe and supple and contributing a sensuality all of her own she simply oozed sexual charisma from every contour, displaying itself in the perfectly proportioned vestige of a girl whose determination to contain her charms from those who sought nothing else but sexual pleasure were without reservation. Her body had been abused, and she could never forget that as she positioned her breasts into a bra that did little to hide the firm fullness that had developed over the years, to posture a reflection that now afforded everything that even a fully grown woman could feel proud of.

Again, apart from her bra she stood naked in an enthused exhilaration to show herself off, though with no onlookers on offer she would have to contend with pirouetting across the floor in a demonstration of her athleticism to a mouse that peeked inquisitively from a crack in the floor panelling. And although still only seventeen, she remained convinced that one day she would find true love. The short, mauve coloured dress that expounded on every little detail of a figure that demanded to be noticed, highlighted the auburn locks that splayed casually across bare shoulders in a demonstrative attempt to catch the ivory texture of her skin. Her facial features still bore the hallmarks of one who had suffered, with large brown eyes opening a world that retained a determination not to be beaten.

Dimpled cheeks etched out the seductive smile with which she would derive great fun in tantalising the younger boys, drawing on their naivety and whose puberty drew them into a world of fantasy, satisfying their wet dreams in simplistic displays of sexual orientations. Her nose was small, with an accumulative display of tiny freckles offering a cuteness that attempted to simplify her glamour, though to do that was certainly something that would prove hard to achieve. Swirling in front of the mirror, she satisfied herself that Tom would be proud of her and keen to show her off to his friends, although his determination to introduce her to his parents would have to wait.

"She was not yet ready for such a confrontation, and in any case, it wouldn't be fair on her mother," she muttered in agreement with her thoughts.

The air was still, with an overpowering fragrance of hollyhock and sweet-pee scenting the early morning mist, swirling in confused abandonment drawn on by the warm currents in an obstinate disregard to the disorientation it caused to the animal kingdom, and of course, the simple human being! It was 2am, and Maria was late home, having promised her mother faithfully she would be no later than 12.30am. Tom had escorted her as far as the post office with her insistence that she could manage the last hundred yards to her front gate, leaving Tom to make his way home concerned and disappointed at her lack of affection towards him throughout the evening. Love didn't come easy!

At first she walked slowly, finding it difficult to see in the increasing mist as picking up speed she stumbled on a flagstone, causing the strap on her shoe to loosen.

"Damn!" she acknowledged, stopping under a streetlight as she stooped to adjust the offending item, her concentration disturbed by the sound of heavy breathing to her rear. Her sense of foreboding increased as each menacing and disconcerting breath infused an overpowering acknowledgement of fearful apprehension and acceptance to her vulnerability. She froze!

Slowly she turned, her eyes focusing in horror as a hand reached out menacingly from the shadows. She went to scream, but her mouth was dry as her whispered vocal chords croaked out a desperate plea for, "mercy!" Without thinking her fingers automatically grasped firmly about the handle of a bag that stood ready to fend off whatever this monster had in store for her.

The hand stretched cautiously towards her shoulder, the breathing increased, louder, consuming and almost screaming at her within a crescendo of sinister decibels. Her body tingled! Goose-pimpled and cold as trembling in fear and trepidation she could feel the weight as fingers long and claw like clamped firmly about the damp flesh covering a body that had almost resigning itself to the inevitable.

An arm followed, gruesome, like an entwining tentacle ready to squeeze the last ounce of oxygen from lungs that felt ready to burst as she held her breath.

Then a shoulder! Broad and menacing, demonic in its entirety and ready to smother her in an embrace of certain death! And then a face! A face that offered a broad and concerned smile and that wished her no harm. It was the face of her brother Peter, dear Peter who had been sent to search for her by her worried parents. Such was her imagination!

She collapsed in his arms sobbing, "You bastard! You fucking bastard! You scared the shit out of me," she cried almost hysterically, her fears of having escaped yet another rape or worse compounded with her relief at finding her beloved brother, here, ready to protect her from all evil. Pounding him on the chest in an almost frenzied display of confusion and terror she offered outbursts of relief and gratitude as both sobbing and laughing she thanked him, thanked him with all her heart.

"Thank God it was you!" she exclaimed, her heartbeat falling though still angry with him for scaring her in such away. She smiled as she relaxed within the warmth and safety of his six foot three frame. "How I love you, you great big fool," she muttered to herself as she snuggled up to him, accepting with gratitude his offer to wipe away her tears.

Her parents were waiting anxiously at the gate having heard her screams though relieved to see her safely in the arms of her brother. Sonny had left her room wearing nothing but a flimsy nightdress, having completely forgotten to snatch her dressing gown in all the commotion, leaving her standing under the streetlight displaying a naked figure through a transparent nightdress that had the neighbours gasping. Her innocence subjected itself to the occasion as she muttered. "Are you OK?" though met with an astonished stare from Maria.

She couldn't help but laugh at her embarrassment as Peter handed her his jacket, with a note of disapproval expressing his annoyance that his own sister could exhibit herself in such a way, and in front of the neighbours! Though looking at her still standing under the streetlight, wretched and forlorn and holding the jacket to her front, he couldn't help but laugh.

David on the other-hand did nothing more than look on from the upstairs window, his face scowled his jealousy overflowing as he watched his 'little Maria' still snuggled up to that brother of his. He showed little concern for her well-being, just an overpowering fit of possessiveness, with his brotherly instincts lost in a haze of infatuation that he'd been fighting with for months. He loved her and that was that, but no one must ever know, he would deal with it in his own way as turning he removed a photograph from his bottom drawer, hidden away under a pile of papers, out of sight but, not out of mind.

With eyes that devoured the subject of his approval his chest tightened, as did his fingers as he trembled with anticipation.

"My sweet Maria," he muttered, "how I wish you were mine." But, the picture was not of some innocent holiday snap or relaxed family moment, no, it was a picture of Maria sunbathing at the bottom of the garden, her skimpy bikini-top removed as she stretched her back in an arched submission to the sun, offering herself to the Gods in the hope of being rewarded with 'a good suntan'.

Her innocent exposure to the sun's rays were offered unconditionally, though little did she realise that she was also offering herself to the zoom of her brother's camera, as pushing her bikini bottom down a little she'd let those very same sun's rays play across her lower abdomen, conveniently highlighting the few silken strands of pubic hairs that had strayed above her bikini-line and something that her brother had eagerly sought to catch on camera. "He would relish that photograph forever!"

With the commotion and concerns over they returned to the cottage. Maria's parents refrained from submitting their feelings at such a late hour, ones that offered dismay more than anger, disappointed at their daughter's obvious lack of concern in disobeying their instructions though fully realising that at seventeen she was almost an adult. Even so, house rules did apply and they would talk with her tomorrow. Maria offered a quick apology as she headed for her bed, dampening their enthusiasm to condemn her actions alongside the fact that neither she nor Tom had remembered their mobiles. This waved slightly in her favour. And! No doubt the shock would teach her a lesson she would never forget!

"But still! A good talking too wouldn't go amiss," exclaimed Amy as she snuggled up to her dear husband of twenty-four years, offering herself to his advances in an amused silence that he should still want her after all this time, and, at 4am in the morning. "Love was a wonderful thing!" she motioned quietly.

David was late for work, and didn't the whole household know it. His bloody car had broken down and the taxi driver was now fifteen minutes late after he'd promised faithfully to get him into Horton by eight thirty. Peter offered to run him there which was rejected out of hand, his innocent embrace with Maria still running strong in his brother's warped mind.

"He could not ignore the fact that the taxi driver might be held up in some traffic jam," was the feeble reasoning given behind his abrupt dismissal of the offer, though glancing at Maria, whose annoyance with his attitude showed, his frustrations grew.

A knock at the door heralded the arrival of the taxi, leaving David to curse the driver in response to which he immediately left.

"He'll be lucky to get a taxi from that company again," muttered Peter under his breath, trying to hide a smile to which his brother scowled, grabbed his briefcase and headed for the bus stop, exclaiming that, "the damn estate agents were lucky to have him working there in the first place." The bus arrived an hour later!

Each busied themselves in their own preparations for the day. Maria had late studies at Moorcroft Collage just outside of Horton and a short bus ride from the village, though Peter would give her a lift on his way to Crowthorp Farm where he worked as 'farm manager'. Sonny wasn't due back at University until Wednesday, and she wanted desperately to spend the day, and the evening, with Andy, licking her lips at the prospect. Tomorrow she would complete her notes and that letter to the 'London fashion House' where she had been offered work.

"If she attained the appropriate degree that was!" she acknowledged with satisfaction, almost sure of success!

David had gone at last, "thank God!" they all nodded in agreement, while Arthur had just a short walk to his 'Den' as he affectionately called it. Amy worked part-time at the village store her hours restricted by an overly concerned Arthur.

"She has enough to do," he insisted, "looking after two strapping lads and two very demanding girls," he'd laughingly exclaimed only last Christmas as he'd hugged both of them in turn.

"And so has your father," Amy had piped up, "but not quite enough," she'd joked, dragging him from the comfort of an easy chair he'd conveniently reserved in front of a roaring fire and showing him the broken drawer he'd promised to fix. And so life went on!

Chapter II

Summer turned to Autumn with life at the cottage offering harmony and security, although David, whose continuing infatuation with his younger sister and sly observations of her dress - or lack of it - as she fritted about in an evening doing her chores, often in her night attire moving in total innocence of those staring eyes that followed her every move, spent more of his spare time mooching about the house. His lack of a steady girlfriend - or any girlfriend for that matter - had not gone unnoticed by the family. His brooding and continuing sarcasm - especially towards Peter - caused increased consternation to his parents, who demanded he get a grip on things, "if it was work that was bothering him?" they questioned in despair.

But it wasn't work! It was that beautiful creature that had just walked past him, swinging her hips in a tantalising gesture of innocent fun as she lent to retrieve the wash basket from the floor. It was no use; he just couldn't help himself as his eyes followed her legs, watching in a mesmerized submission to his feelings as her back arched towards the scattering of fallen garments littering the carpet.

He followed her movements quietly, watching carefully as the short, tightly fitting skirt rose sharply to just beneath her buttocks, offering just the slightest of glimpses of her white collage-knickers. It was all too much for David, as hot under the collar he tried to look away. He couldn't! He could only stare in fascination and lust as Maria turned her head to face him, tormenting, smiling with one of those demurring smiles that sent the blood rushing to his head.

"OK?" she smiled again. No response, so she continued.

Her hand reached further for a pair of socks that eluded her, her back arching still further as desperately her fingers strained to reach "those damn things", offering little concern as her skirt rose consistent to each move her innocence unremitting as the clefs of each cheek came into view. At that point Peter entered the room, slapping her bottom to laughingly remind her, "What delightful cheeks she was displaying." Blushing she stood up, but not before noticing David's eyes focused intently on her behind, his face unmoving his eyes wide and staring, clenching his fist in an almost uncontrollable desire to see more.

"Are you OK?" she asked him once again, concerned at such strange behaviour. He nodded unconsciously, his eyes following the contours of a figure that offered everything he had ever wanted in a girl as again she enquired. "Are you sure?"

For a moment he remained puzzled, then shaking his head he smiled back that of course he was. "Just a touch of migraine," he murmured holding his head, glancing at Peter from the corner of one eye. "Thank God he hadn't realised, nor had Maria," he sighed as they offered consoling references to his condition. "But he must be careful!"

The village was holding a 'self sufficiency day' in respect of raising funds to purchase a fifteen acre chunk of farmland where cultivation could take place, offering the villagers the chance to invest in their own 'home grown' produce. Local farmers had raised no objection as long as the villagers continued to purchase their dairy products, to include most of their beef, pork and lamb. Poultry was a flexible issue, and with just a number of smaller problems that needed ironing out the whole enterprise appeared quite a conceivable and practical proposition.

Arthur was in a dilemma; he'd been approached by the organising committee to consider the restoration of the workings of the mill, and, with a suggestion of financial support in the process.

"He was certain to require a lot more financial help than anything they could offer," he queried with Amy insistently, "although the idea in itself certainly seems worthy of consideration," he mused confidently, satisfied that he was quite capable of achieving such an undertaking. "After all, the mill is in excellent condition, with everything intact though the foundations would have to be seen too, also the wheel, with at least two of the wooden supports and a varying number of slats, cogs, nuts, and bolts," he continued to an enthused Amy, who was keen to offer him every support for such an enterprising venture.

"Still, apart from the finance there appears to be few problems, and the venture itself could ensure a sizable return. In theory at least!" he hastened to add. For a time he deliberated such a move, though his mind was made up, and in informing the committee that he was certainly interested - not just for himself but for the benefit of the whole project - he was offered a grant of £6,000, with a further £4,000 interest free loan over three years. Though the inclusion of 10% of his profits over that very same period wasn't quite as attractive!

Arthur scratched his head, whilst acknowledging that his thoughts must demand that there should be a positive response. "The amount on offer will come nowhere near the estimated £25,000 for the job as a whole, though with £15,000 from our own savings the problem could be solved," he motioned to the now confused Amy, who was by no means a mathematical genius, nor anything near it.

"Of course dear," she murmured, "though it does sound rather extortionate," having no idea what she was talking about but keen to sound enthusiastic, offering solidarity and support to any little venture he decided to undertake.

"However, there was still the loan to repay and that 10% off our profits, that's if of course we make a profit!" he pondered, looking at Amy for some notification of approval, or otherwise! She smiled! Hugging him and telling him to go ahead!

"They will all help!" she reassured him. Though she had her doubts!

The late autumn storms blew relentlessly, stripping the surviving leaves from their protective branches with an eagerness to remind them that winter was on the doorstep and that they had no right to be there. The fields had been harvested leaving them bare and cold, with the owl and kestrel searching for easy pickings in stubble that offered little in the way of shelter. The rain beat mercilessly on earth already saturated, flooding the low-lying areas in a heartless gesture of defiance to any puny defences erected during the summer for such an occasion. Winter was indeed on the doorstep, and as such Mother Nature had decided that an early reminder would convince a world that organised its life within a seasonal timetable that preparations for a hard winter should be high on the agenda.

Maria stared from her bedroom window in dismay, watching the rain splattering against the glass panels with each belligerent gust of wind tormenting her spirit as she endeavoured to focus to the far end of the driveway; a driveway from where she expected to see the arrival of her dear Tom whom she hoped would at last be accepted by her overly concerned mother. He had been invited for dinner and his first encounter with her family as a group, although individually he had been introduced to all five ages ago.

Ten minutes lapsed, then fifteen as Maria continued to scan the area of her concern, and then, a hapless Tom appeared from out of the murk, holding on frantically to an umbrella that had long since ceased to be anything else but a perilous rebuff to nature's inspired insistence on giving him a resounding soaking.

He had made it, although his lack of enthusiasm to meet Maria's mother - informally this time - gave him every justification to offer every excuse under the sun to abstain from such an encounter. Maria was waiting at the door as a drenched Tom clawed his way through the howling wind and driving rain, finally to relinquish his hold on his umbrella, watching it disappear across the garden, hover for a moment as it crossed a thick covering of shrubs and bushes, narrowly missing an elderly lady, eventually to lay in a mangled heap on the road. The wheel from a passing car had seen to its demise! They both laughed, leaving Tom to insist that his sister's umbrella was no less a protective device against the elements than that of King Chanute's demands that the seas retreat from his person. "HE nearly drowned!"

A quick kiss from Maria lightened his spirits as he peered through the lounge doorway to confront this marauding pack of wolves that awaited his arrival with an eagerness to pass moral judgement on his character before devouring him. It was not to be, with Arthur's welcome more akin to that of a father as shaking his hand he remarked, "good to see you my boy!" embracing him like the long lost prodigal son, much to Tom's embarrassment.

Dear Peter strode forward with as much enthusiasm, offering his hand and a pat on the back and announcing, "so we meet again, always good to see you mate," no less the gentleman and as cheerful as ever.

Sonny lurched towards him – after first tripping on that damn cat – like an adoring metaphor of some long lost love whose prayers had been answered as she embraced him with a passion that had poor Tom reeling. "Good to see you darling, and…!" she whispered, to which she was speedily dragged off by a laughing Maria, whose attempts at scolding her erupted into fits of laughter.

David didn't move, he just nodded with his disapproval obvious as turning away he continued with his reading of the paper. Maria glared at him furiously, wondering why he was behaving in such a manner and convinced that for whatever reason he chose he was just, downright jealous!

"Perhaps it would explain why she had noticed him peeping at her through the partly open bedroom door the other week, as she was preparing for bed!" she considered angrily, although to actually prove such a suggestion was something else. She had been naked, naked and unassuming, brushing her hair in front of the mirror, the same mirror attached to her dressing table that had reflected his face as she picked out a pair of wide staring eyes; eyes that focused on her bottom in a mesmerized display of pure lust.

"And, just like that time she'd been preparing the washing in the lounge and she'd caught him staring at her then," she mused despairingly, a feeling of disgust bordering on revulsion causing her to shiver.

"He definitely has a problem!" she muttered angrily. She glared at him again, though without a word as she caught sight of Tom leaning over her mother, her smile saying it all as Tom offered her a little kiss on the cheek.

"Why, the crafty bugger has won her over," she chuckled in an adoring admiration of his tactics. "Wait 'till I get my hands on the crafty fu...!" Remembering where she was she held her mouth, such language certainly wouldn't be appreciated by her parents.

The evening went well, leaving Tom a popular and accepted member of a family gathering that preferred to forget his rather dubious past, reflecting more on what they were confronted with and not with a reputation that now superseded him.

The ease in which Tom had settled into the atmosphere of the situation dispelled any concerns Maria could possibly have had that her mother would never accept him. On the contrary, her laughing and joking with this hansom young man could almost be interpreted as a form of flirtation. Amy was certainly no dowdy old mother figure. At forty-three she remained stunningly attractive, leaving girls almost half her age wishing that they too could have a figure that offered everything that most men would be more than happy with, and, that any young girl would be proud of. She worked out at the local gym' twice weekly, taking every care into seeing that she retained that youthful look and ensuring that her figure would endure such hardships as age slowly eroded such youth.

Her life had become stagnant and sexually wanting, having never experienced anything in life that might be considered as something 'bordering on an affair', with her only recognition of 'a real sexual experience' being a quick flirtation with a nineteen-year old boy in the sports club shower-room.

It was a year ago almost to the day that they had found themselves alone after a late 'work-out', although it remained questionable whether a further 'work out' had been something that either had the inclination or the desire to pursue. Oblivious to Amy's presence the unsuspecting young man had unwittingly made his way into the steamy interior of the ladies locker-room to retrieve the towel he had left behind just fifteen minutes earlier It was of course the wrong room, as turning to leave his eye caught the naked outline of Amy soaping herself down in a shower cubical, complete in her innocence that such circumstances would never attract anyone never mind the attentions of this young man.

How wrong could she be, with her initial shock and embarrassment soon melting at the insistence from this mature and rather pensive Casanova that she had nothing to worry about, something that had certainly been the case as they'd made love! She had relished every moment of this 'physical enlightenment' as his young body had consumed her with a passion and excitement that had left her gasping, with only her feelings of guilt for her beloved Arthur preventing her from seeing him again. His agitation at such a terminal dismissal had left her wondering!

Having lost herself in this world of mystical illusion and fantasy for a while her eyes reflected the feeling of that intimate moment as she gazed adoringly into Tom's dark, sensuous eyes; eyes that quickly reminded her who HE was, and, where SHE was as she sank back into her chair.

"Damn!" she muttered. "Damn! Damn!" having decided that she was in the wrong place at the wrong time, "though not with the wrong person," she smiled ruefully.

Her obvious feelings for him had not gone unnoticed by Tom, who was always prepared to accept a challenge, "especially with his girlfriend's mother," he smiled secretly to himself. "And what a mother," he smirked as his eyes focused on her low-cut dress, admiring breasts that flaunted themselves in his direction, inviting him to venture into the depths of her soul leaving Tom little in the way of discouragement. In effect, her adventuress flirtations offered Tom everything in the way of encouragement! She had been drinking! And so had Tom, as he paid her more attention than one might have expected from her daughter's boyfriend.

Maria glanced at them both in annoyance, as did Arthur, who although easy going and liberal in his thinking could still see that his wife was flirting with Tom, and, that Tom was reciprocating!

"He would talk to her later," he angered, not wanting to ruin the evening but never the less determined that he wouldn't be made a spectacle of.

Sonny was also experiencing problems! Big ones! James had rung to cancel their next date the evening following, offering some feeble excuse that his mother had insisted that as she had a spare ticket for a concert at the Royal theatre in Exmouth to see a rendering of Gilbert and Sullivan's 'The Pirates of Penzance', he should join her. He would be doing no such thing, and she knew it.

"It would be that horrible women - the one with the big boobs and loins that seemingly oozed attention – that he'd introduced her too at a party, and the one who had spent most of the evening throwing herself at him that would be the most likely candidate for his excuse" she muttered angrily, trying hard to conceal the hurt she was enduring. A row had ensued leaving Sonny in tears, insisting that, "that horrible creature wouldn't be able to give him as good a fuck as she could, and, that her boobs would most probably smother him and hopefully would for all she cared". Maria had heard every word as she prepared black coffee in the kitchen, determined to try and sober up Tom and her mother before her father, and she, 'lost it completely'.

Their behaviour had exceeded the realms in which black coffee would have any effect. Any effect whatsoever, they were both drunk! Maria's attempts at consoling her sister had Sonny insisting, "That she couldn't be left alone through the night," and, "that she had to talk to someone," and, "that someone had to be her. Otherwise she'd kill herself!" she sobbed, more concerned with the indignity of it all than anything else. "After all, who was he to call the shots, she could take her pick!" she acknowledged in satisfaction, her continuing outburst of tears and whispered obscenities reflecting nothing less than self-pity.

Maria agreed, though her defined amusement at her dear Sonny's refusal to accept that 'it was over' and, that deep-down her sister 'couldn't give a toss', left her sighing in exasperation, indicating that, "she would be up later, after she had sorted out that bloody mess," pointing to Tom and her mother, who had now resorted to smooching. Right in front of her father!

Arthur sat fuming, his patience with his wife and Tom having almost exhausted itself as Peter moved hesitantly towards his mother, unable to dismiss his father's annoyance at her antics any longer, leaving him concerned and angered having followed all three with some degree of trepidation. His father had - on more than one occasion - displayed a fit of temper that had worried him, and now he was concerned for his mother whose inane ramblings could only make matters worse.

"Perhaps you should spend tonight with Maria mother, just to be on the safe side!" he insisted, taking her arm carefully and helping her to her feet.

"And a bloody good idea!" his father agreed, his face flushed with a level of anger that he now found difficult to control as he left them to it, though not without one more observation. "And as for Tom, he's not in any fit state to go anywhere, look at the idiot!" he remarked to a now very concerned Peter, having left his mother for a moment and who had now prepared for the worst as his father pointed to a Tom who would appear to consider Amy as his own, with his hands everywhere and totally oblivious to his surroundings.

"Just keep him out of my way," Arthur motioned to his son. "And I think perhaps it's for the best that he spends the night on the bloody sofa," he fumed, his face contorting with each angered syllable as he spoke. "I'll deal with him tomorrow!" he growled under his breath.

So! The evening that had started out so well had now finished in disaster, leaving Maria to slap Tom across the face implying that she would never speak to him again, and, that their relationship was finished.

"You've just succeeded in making a bloody fool of me, and insulting my father in the process," she shouted as he slumped to the floor in a heap, forcing the black coffee - which was still hot - into his mouth as she attempted to sober him up. The hot coffee certainly went a long way into achieving that aim as spluttering the burning beverage from his mouth he stared at her in astonishment, stunned that she had intentionally tried to burn him.

"Think yourself lucky, the way I feel I'd like to bloody well do a lot more than that," she retorted, her eyes enflamed as storming off she shouted, "and you'd better make a bloody bed up on the sofa, and stay put. Or!" she exclaimed angrily, slamming the door behind her.

David on the other hand had remained silent throughout, watching the proceedings partly in amusement with a continuing anger and frustration that his dear Maria could be bothered with such a useless and inconsiderate fool such as Tom.

"She deserved better," he snarled, convinced that once Tom was out of the way she would perhaps show him more understanding, and, a little affection, though his idea of affection was notably dubious. His resentment of Tom grew as he followed his attempts in preparing the sofa with increasing anger and frustration, the definite of his rage resounding within each syllable as he derided and belittled his antics. Even so, though still disorientated from the drink Tom still managed to do a reasonable job!

Looking up at David with a stupid grin he acknowledged his presence, slurring his words as he remarked, "have a splendid bud light!" to immediately collapse in a heap on the sofa. David scowled back, intent on dealing with this clown once the opportunity arose.

"He would ensure that the fool didn't bother Maria again!" he muttered to himself inconsolably.

Leaving Tom to his dreams he headed for his room, making for the side-draw as he removed that photo from beneath the papers, his eyes focusing on her beauty his mind having already undressed her as he lay back on the bed pondering his next move.

"Perhaps he should try talking to her tonight," he mused carefully, "why she was in such a bad mood with Tom. He would announce his concerns at the way he had behaved and perhaps offer a sympathetic shoulder to cry on," he smiled. He knew he was pushing his luck! "Still!" he acknowledged unconcerned, though his imagination was running wild his anger increasing by the minute as he dwelt on the idea of that buffoon lying in a naked embrace with his beloved Maria. "Revenge would be sweet!" he announced carefully.

Tom had sobered a little though his thoughts were still confused. "His mind was playing tricks! Did he really try to 'chat up' Maria's mother," he wondered to himself, his fuzzed memory turning towards Maria's reaction as he glanced at the coffee stain on his shirt. "She was certainly mad," he pondered in amusement, "and her mother! She was something else," he smirked as he fell into a world of fantasy and lustful desire, to picture her naked on the bed lying ready for his advances in an enthused commitment to enjoy. Shaking off such an enjoyable visionary experience his thoughts concentrated on the present, that of Maria's anger and his wish to make amends.

"Perhaps he should creep up to Maria's room and apologise," he wondered with a smile, convinced that she would forgive him. "And then!" he smiled. "Why, it was almost two o'clock and the rest of the family were sure to be asleep," he agreed. "He would go right now, after all, what had he got to lose!" he smiled confidently.

Maria had returned to her room to find her mother fast asleep, fully dressed lying stretched across the bed in an alcoholic suppression to her instincts. There was no point in trying to wake her as putting on the side lamp and closing the door she proceeded to undress the unremitting Amy, removing her outer garments with military precision leaving her with just bra and knickers though deciding instead to remove both as the alcohol had soaked right through.

"That smell," she muttered holding her nose. "What to do!" she mused in acknowledgement to her mother's predicament as the alcoholic fumes wafted inconsiderately about her face. Having solved the problem she returned with a damped sponge and carefully wiped the offending areas, for a moment allowing herself an admiring glance at a body that certainly didn't show its age, with firm breasts and a slim waist doing credit to the many years of ensuring that age would not dig deep, helped emphatically with the hard work she'd put in at the gym.

For a moment her mother stirred, calling Arthur as she rolled to her side, her eyes flickering as she focused on the blurred spectre of her daughter's indistinct appearance through the casting shadows of a dimmed lamp that appeared to play tricks with her vision.

Maria reassured her by whispering, "I'm OK! I'm sleeping with you this evening and I'll explain tomorrow, but for the moment I have to spend some time with Sonny. She was very, very upset!" She retorted melodramatically, kissing her on the cheek with a "Goodnight mother!" Turning off the lamp she left her mother in total darkness, acknowledging her apologies with a grunt as she attempted to reach the door, though determined that the morning would offer more than just an apology from them both. For a moment her anger softened as she found herself unable to resist a slight smile as she pictured Tom's shocked face at having thought she'd deliberately burnt him.

"Well! Perhaps she just had," she chuckled with conviction.

Ensuring the coast was clear Tom crept steadfastly up the narrowing and seemingly ever-ending staircase; a staircase that seemed to purposely squeak on receipt of each step as if ensuring that his arrival would not go unnoticed, his energies reflected in his desire to convince Maria that he had only been fooling about and that his efforts to offer a good impression to her mother had obviously rebounded. Softly knocking on a door that had eased open ever so slightly, and as if expecting his early arrival, Tom cautiously entered the room.

"Maria! Maria, are you awake?" he questioned softly, in anticipation of a torrent of abuse and without waiting for a reply as warily he edged towards the bed. The room remained in shadowy darkness as closing the door he shuffled towards the bed, tapping the shoulder of Amy whispering, "And have I been forgiven?"

Amy stirred in her sleep, her eyes unable to focus as she welcomed Maria back in a hushed voice with a slurred, "come to bed, and what the hell am I doing in YOUR room?"

Tom stared at her in bewilderment, his glazed eyes seeking some form of solace from the dark as he stroked her hair. "It's Tom!" he announced, "come to apologise," he hastily remarked, awaiting the wrath of God to reap vengeance on his soul. It was not to be as silently she took his hand, placing it firmly on her breast in a gesture of defiance to her husband she remained surprised at the insistence, the cheek of this young man's intention to devour her with a passion and consummation that she eagerly sought.

"A moment Tom, a moment," she whispered unsteadily, uncertain as how to respond though certain of one thing. He would not be disappointed! She knew exactly what this young man had in mind, and she would ensure that his time and hers would not be wasted. Tom remained jubilant, fully convinced that Maria had forgiven him, and now, "wanted to make love to him!"

He undressed, quickly, his mind and body now fully awake to his good fortune as he endeavoured to climb into a bed that simply wouldn't stay still, eventually to be guided by an excited Amy onto a body, although slightly fuller than Maria's, offered all the characteristics and collective anatomic anecdotes that had seen her through premarital defiance to societies moral code, and, that were necessary for her next move.

"Darling!" she whispered, her head clearing rapidly as her back arched in anticipation of Tom's surprisingly erect penis, awaiting its arrival in a consumed passion of over enthusiasm as her hands pulled impatiently at his shoulders.

"Darling!" she whispered again, only this time with a sigh as she drew this monster intrusion to her well-being deep inside the awaiting orifice that closed in a moist reciprocal of desire around it.

"Fuck me hard!" she whispered, her passions devouring Tom in a lustful abandonment of any regret she may have felt as she twisted and turned in a masochistic endeavour to seek to its full this hard, warm delight that was offering her so much pleasure.

"Fuck me harder! she mouthed in a suppressed scream, her breasts pressed closely to his face as she reached forward her hips pressing firmly to his to ensure maximum enjoyment.

And still Tom remained convinced that he was making love to Maria, though her body appeared much softer, her breasts fuller and her loins certainly more demanding since the occasion of their last encounter. An encounter which had only been the once and at the time of her eighteenth birthday! It hadn't been a resounding success as her mind still reflected back to her childhood, and, "those horrible fucking people" she would insist on calling them, her attempts at satisfying his lust failing abysmally. "But tonight, tonight she was putting on the performance of her life!"

A full moon shone down in a benign acknowledgement that the light it offered would finally penetrate the slight gap between the curtains, presenting Tom with the outline of a figure that confused him. Dark shadows played across features that in comparison to the delicate and ivory textured skin of Maria had shown coarseness, with a sallow complexion extending to breasts that highlighted a slightly softer appearance as they drooped - ever so slightly - towards hips that worked energetically in a seemingly unrelenting determination to extract every last ounce of passion still exuberating from loins that attached themselves like limpets to his masculinity.

Her thighs had filled to ones that although offered limited understanding, still managed to entwine themselves about his person in an exotic entrapment not to relinquish this monolith to an experience only exceeded by her encounter last year. Her moans and sighs had an element of huskiness that convinced Tom once and for all that if it wasn't Maria whose arched back lay before him, "then who the hell was it?"

Facing the window her buttocks rose in anticipation to her demands, her mind exploding into a torrent of wishful thinking as Tom urgently endeavoured to take stock of a situation that totally confused him.

"Who in hell's name was he fucking," he mused in astonishment as he felt a firm grip to his penis, gasping as it disappeared between cheeks that clenched tightly about this gesture of goodwill.

He would never find out! Never, as his body sank across Amy's back in a limp detachment from reality, his head smashed into several pieces as the force of the blow shattered his skull without recrimination or remorse.

He would never know! As the blood oozed from a gash that had penetrated the brain, with a mixture of grey matter and gung excreting from his nose and mouth as his soulless eyes stared at a face that he most certainly would have recognised.

And! He would never again see the person he had just been making love too, his face now devoid of expression, with features that hung grotesquely from cheekbones distorting an appearance that had consumed many a girl in a passionate embrace, though now offering little more than the devil's embodiment of a mortal that had ceased to be as his head lolled towards the shadowy figure that was quickly heading for the door. A head unrecognisable in its entirety, and that offered a last gesture of defiance to its demise as it faced a figure that insisted on closing the bedroom door tightly, with just a simple thud!

The household awoke to the echoing screams that pierced the still night air with an intensity that convinced the resident wildlife that hell had at last delivered its tortured souls to exact vengeance on their very being. To extradite them from the comforts of a garden that offered everything to their very survival, and, to a world where life held hardships untold.

An owl hooted in the distance in an acceptance that not all was right with the world, demanding to know what all the commotion was about as Peter arrived on the scene, his astonishment evident as he witnessed the naked figure of his mother struggling to remove the body of Tom from a back that had now relented under the pressure, infusing torment on breasts that shook with the effort extracted from a body now weary and sore from a multitude of intrusions.

Her hysterical screams dissociated themselves from a bottom offering an unsympathetic view of pubic bush as leaning forwards she extracted Tom's body from her person. In one! Last! Heroic effort! Without care or awareness she leant still further, her mortal being expounding into an unremitting acknowledgement to her nudity, and offering an unreserved view of all that had entered into holy accord with a Tom now dead and immortalised only in the spirit world.

Her crazed eyes searched for sanctuary as she persisted in her endeavours to remove his corpse from the bed, leaving Peter to hide his obvious embarrassment as quickly coming to her aid he covered her nakedness with a sheet. His arms offered the soothing and consoling that she so desired as she sobbed unreservedly into his chest, her hands reaching for his face as she whispered soulfully, "Tom tried to rape me!" Continuing with, "then someone murdered him! I saw him from the corner of my eye! A horrible shadowy creature," she murmured, her voice trembling in a terrifying recognition of the situation she'd just encountered.

Maria had followed Peter, her own screams blending into a concerto of anguish as she surveyed the scene in disbelief, her mind recoiling in horror on identifying the mutilated body of Tom from behind the bed as her eyes searched incongruously for some sign of a murder weapon that didn't necessarily exist. The sight of her mother whimpering in Peter's arms with the sheet now having worked its way forlornly to her waist in an uncompromising attempt to reveal more, displaying whelps and bruises that would have been more than enough to convince any unsuspecting person that, "Yes! She had been raped!" Did little to convince Maria!

"Though to actually murder Tom was way out of her mother's league," she persisted, in a belief that she just wouldn't be capable of such a thing. For a moment her thoughts focused on her mother's dignity as she sprang to her rescue, securing the sheet with two safety pins as her father arrived, speedily followed by a Sonny who in all the confusion had completely forgotten that she had got out of bed wearing just her knickers, arriving half asleep and oblivious to the fact that her naked breasts were now pressing hard against her father's back as she attempted to peer over his shoulder to see what all the fuss was about.

Maria threw her a towel, her finger pointing at her own breasts as she tried to draw Sonny's attention to her semi-nakedness, whispering, "You forgot to dress! You're almost naked!" To a totally unconcerned Sonny as smirking she rapped the towel about the offending objects. "She didn't care!"

The last to arrive was of course David, sauntering into the room as casually he glanced over to the body. He nodded his disapproval with a grimace muttering, "shame!" as he stared indifferently towards his mother, trying not to smile at her predicament as once again that blasted safety pin loosened itself to expose his mother's now familiar breasts; breasts that once again offered themselves unconditionally though in a less than dignified manner. Slowly the sheet sank to the floor as his mother continued unperturbed to expound on her innocence to all and sundry, causing David to snigger in disgust as he left the room.

"He had seen enough," he remarked unconcerned, explaining that, "he would return when the police arrived. He was tired!"

Arthur wasted no time in informing the police of poor Tom's gruesome death, with the officer insisting that the body shouldn't be touched and that they should all remain in the room. David was summoned back immediately, complaining of lack of sleep and that he had a heavy day at the office awaiting him. No one took the slightest bit of notice at his concerns as they waited patiently for the police, with Amy repeatedly reminding them all that she'd been raped and, that she was innocent of any killing. It took Peter, Maria, and Sonny to calm her, insisting that they believed her and that she hadn't a problem, though Arthur remained seated, "unsure of anything!"

A knock at the door heralded the arrival of the police as Detective Chief Inspector Alan Lawson introduced himself as, "a man who never lost a case, and liked to see all the loose ends neatly tied together, quickly!"

"We will do our best to help sir," Arthur assured him as he directed the two policemen and one policewoman to the scene of the crime. A further knock at the door introduced three forensic officers followed by a doctor.

"All eager to get the job over as quickly as possible, as they'd had a busy night!" was voiced in quick accord, having accepted that here was a situation readily solved.

"You will of course be lent our every assistance, with full co-operation by everyone, including David," he remarked cynically, allowing his voice to rise slightly having ignored his son's protest with a look of indifference.

Interviews took place individually in Sonny's room, while the forensic team tried hard to uncover anything that might relate to the crime, taking fingerprints and blood samples for DNA analysis later. The doctor didn't hesitate in pronouncing Tom dead, exacting a time of death as between 12am and 3am from the body's condition. His ascertain wasn't required as Amy knew, "exactly the time of his death," her whispered voice rising into a crescendo as she announced that, "she'd fucking well been there!"

The Inspector looked at her in astonishment, especially when once again the sheet decided that hanging precariously from little more than a thread was preferable to the covering of that of a woman whose body could demand a considerable degree of attention as both pins sprang lose, to offer him a display of feminine charms as her breasts expressed themselves unconditionally in an unassuming display of eroticism. Unwittingly she attempted to rescue the sheet from the floor, assisted to the obvious embarrassment by a policeman whose evident delight at being confronted with a full bush of pubic hairs staring him in the face turned sour as he found himself quickly admonished by the Inspector.

Composing himself within the confounds of one whose lifelong vocation had been to uphold the law, the Inspector then went on to inform Amy that she could be incriminating herself if she continued with her recount of everything that, "she thought had taken place." And! "To think carefully before she spoke again."

Further questioning proved pointless! No one had heard anything! No one had seen anything - apart from Amy that was - and no one had the slightest idea who the murderer might be.

"Though suspicion must certainly fall on David," were concerns paramount in Maria's mind. "After all, he certainly detested Tom, having embarked in an embittered demonstration of obsessive ness towards her," she recounted grimly. "And his mood swings, and the string of aggressive remarks all undoubtedly displayed a mind that could certainly snap if pushed to the limits."

David ignored their discerning glances, quite content to, "let them think what the bloody hell they liked," as, "he wasn't the culprit!"

"Their father had certainly been more than angry with Tom," were thoughts dwelling on the minds of his children. "Though even with his occasional outbursts of temper he surely wouldn't be capable of killing anyone, would he?" they each acknowledged secretively, though unwilling to accept such outlandish observations.

"Would he? Would he was certainly a question worth consideration," decided Maria as she pondered for a moment, though not fully convinced with her assumptions. "Surely not!" she remained persuaded as she dwelt for a moment on the kindly though perhaps deceivingly pacify face of her adored father. He smiled at her reassuringly!

An hour past, leaving the forensic team both dejected and frustrated. "Not even a hair or a single thread to work on," their muttered grunts sounding their continued frustration. "Or one drop of the murderer's blood from perhaps a scratch," was the sullen announcement. "But they had found traces of soil and clay reaching from the door to the bed, although no footprints, and, there were no further traces outside of the bedroom." They remained baffled, offering a simple explanation that, "perhaps the intruder took his muddy shoes of before entering the premises, then having climbed the stairs decided for some unknown reason to wear them again, in the bedroom!"

"Idiots!" muttered Maria, her eyes following their every move her annoyance contained at such stupid deductions.

There appeared little more to go on, just Amy's insistence that the killer, or, "this strange shadowy thing," as she so aptly defined it, had defiantly retreated through the slightly open doorway. "She had seen the thing as she was trying to fiend off Tom's vicious attack," she lied! To which the Inspector with a smirk rather unwisely asked her, "If it was wearing shoes?"

Amy's response was in accordance with her feelings, leaving her quick to reply with, "and how the hell do I know you sarcastic bastard, I was being raped at the time you fucking imbecile," as once again she secured the sheet, only this time ensuring that it would remain intact to her still trembling body, leaving the smirk to quickly disappear from the Inspector's embarrassed face.

Deciding that further questioning would be necessary, and, probably down at the station, he oversaw the removal of Tom's body to an awaiting ambulance, indicating that a pathologist's report would shed more light on the situation.

"They were not to leave the house for the next twenty-four hours," exclaimed the Inspector, to which David remarked, "that he would most probably get the f…in sack if he missed work once again." The Inspector acknowledged his concern with a nod, reminding him to watch his language, especially in front of his mother, and to get some sleep. "He would most probably have a nice little chat with him in the afternoon, and, at the station," he concluded. David scowled!

Three weeks had past with a string of fresh questions being thrown at the family, though with investigations further afield shedding little light on a situation that proved increasingly difficult to comprehend. Tom had had his enemies, but not one who had been considered evil or bothered enough to kill him.

"Anyhow, how would anyone have known that he was in Maria's room, and, that he was in the process of raping her mother!" muttered the Inspector to his watch, as he realised it would soon be lunchtime.

"There remained just four people in the whole wide world who were aware of the fact that Amy would be sleeping in her room. Arthur, Sonny, Peter and of course, Maria! Only David including Tom would obviously assume that Maria would be alone in her own room."

He rubbed his stomach, "steak and chips would do nicely thank you," he smiled impatiently as again he looked at his watch. "If it wasn't a family member, as it would appear, then it had to be an intruder. An intruder who had some idea of the layout of the place, hadn't startled the animals, didn't appear to have footprints, and, didn't portray an obvious motive for the killing!" he motioned to the clock on the wall. "Ten minutes to go!" he exclaimed, licking his lips in anticipation.

"Confusion, Confusion!" Muttered the Inspector, scratching his head as he raked his brains for any semblance of reasoning that might come to mind, his frustration mounting as he continued to search through notes and files, photos and a host of Internet information, but still coming up with a blank. He had never lost a case before, but now! Three times the Detective Chief Inspector - alongside two of his comrades - had returned to the scene of the crime, with soil analysis at least proving one thing, that the area of the mill was a possible source of this particular type of deep clay soil.

Again the Inspector racked his brains, for anything! "Any bloody thing that would shed some light on this fiasco," he groaned. "And almost one o'clock with just three minutes to go," he scowled, looking at his watch again as if some divine inspiration would be forthcoming from the dial. There was none!

Over and over again questions still unresolved flooded his brain. "Recent exploratory excavations for the reconstruction to the mill's foundations had uncovered this unusual substance, and now it had mysteriously appeared in an area between a door and a bed, in Maria's room, and at the time of a horrendous murder. And nowhere else! Not even the outside mud grid where one might have expected the removal of his boots." He remained confused!

"Bugger this," he snarled, "I'm off to lunch!" It was twenty past one!

Time went by, with an open verdict being offered for Tom's death, "Though if any fresh evidence arose the case would immediately be reopened," Tom's grief stricken parents were quickly reassured by the Judge, his face offering conciliation his slight smile an understanding at their dissatisfaction with the findings.

Chapter III

As the months went by once again harmony reigned in the Martin residence. Arthur was back to his old jovial self having decided that to believe in his wife and accept that she had actually been raped was the better part of valour. He was prepared to turn a blind eye to any suggestion that, 'She might actually have enjoyed it'! "As after all, she was his wife!" he'd concluded dogmatically.

Sonny remained her usual scatterbrain, sexually motivated self, having passed the appropriate exams to enter her into the field of fashion design and modelling, her five foot nine inches and 'fuller women's figure' offering more than enough for a varying assortment of photographers to get excited about. Some with dubious intentions, "though if the money was right she wasn't particularly bothered whether she had to pose naked or otherwise," she smiled wickedly to Maria, whose pretence at shock on hearing such a statement had them both bursting into fits of laughter.

"It was all a learning process," she would laughingly remind Maria as she demonstrated her modelling techniques, leaving Maria gasping in disbelief at her effrontery as leaning back in a naked repose her more than ample breasts defied the laws of gravity in balancing innocuously under her chin.

"Clever stuff!" applauded the enthused Maria, finding herself unable to calculate what her dear sister would do next. "How she loved her!"

Peter extended his ambitions in the field of farming management, with a number of enterprising 'working holidays' in Holland and Germany, initiating several schemes that would offer considerable benefit to the European farming community as a whole. He was now engaged! Having involved himself with an adoring girl of exceptional beauty whose family connections could only enhance his prospects. Her father owned a substantial dairy and agricultural farm of five hundred acres, with one hundred and fifty head of cattle and a thriving breeding policy.

"Not that this had any bearing on his love for this gorgeous, blond, blue-eyed beauty," he had announced to the family, his father giving him an approving wink in an acceptance of his initiative.

David on the other hand had excelled in nothing. He had been sacked from his estate agents job after continuing absenteeism, spending an increasing amount of time hanging about the house, and, spying on Maria. His camera had seemingly devised a way of peering through every crack imaginable, having found some exceptional pictures of Maria parading naked in the bathroom as she determined whether or not her breasts had increased in size since her nineteenth birthday and, that perhaps an inch or two could be removed from her bottom. Her figure remained perfect!

The camera had not been wanting in its determination to personalise her private life, as explicit takes of intimate moments with her new boyfriend had promised David hours of unremitting excitement.

"He could wait!" he muttered, his mind eroded within the confines of increasing frustration that sexual intercourse with Maria or anything resembling such lucrative delights hadn't come his way.

"Perhaps an alternative approach would prove more successful," his crazed mind had demanded. "Anything was preferable to this continuing torment to his soul!" he announced to his favourite photo, his lips pressed hard against the topless body of Maria as he replaced it in the drawer. "He couldn't wait!"

Maria had taken up a post as a nanny, having declined the opportunity to enter into university life insisting, "That a level of practical work should offer her a more rewarding return on an investment in a life that demanded that she repay some of her good fortunes with a degree of self-sacrifice." Though her idea of 'self-sacrifice' might be deemed as rather a fortuitous statement by those who considered a nanny's job as one attaining to that of a more vocational opportunity! Still!

Her new boyfriend Harry, had enlisted everything she could have wanted in a man of twenty-five – or of any age for that matter - with a string of credentials that even Sonny had envied at as she'd admired his Adonis build from afar, drooling at the enormous 'pay-packet' that forced the crutch of his swimming trunks to go way beyond the realms of durability and offering slightly more than, "just a good evening out!"

"Perhaps sisterly love could be taken too far," she queried as she felt the fullness of 'that packet' sink deeply between her loins. In her dreams! "All's fair in love and war," she smiled in an admission to herself that Harry was, "fair game!"

Amy had retreated to within the family boundaries, busying herself with an increasing inventory of household chores having relinquished her job in the shop. Offering herself as the perfect wife, and in her own way - as atonement for her involvement in poor Tom's death -ensuring that Arthur's sex-life would be as enjoyable as her experiences with the two young men she'd consummated her sexual desires with. Arthur still had a lot to learn, and now she felt that finally she'd attained a renewed though unresolved post marital experience to teach him.

The work on the mill's foundations had posed few problems, though with the discovery by workmen of human bones buried deep within the clay and rock deposits, a feeling of suspense had ensued as they deliberated what their next move should be. Deciding that as work - and therefore pay - could be brought to a standstill, to leave well alone would be their best policy, showing scant regard to their origin as they'd continued with their digging. And in doing so, offered the opportunity to a very excited dog that had strayed too near a chance to steal one of these savoury delights. The appreciative dog had wasted no time, as grinding its jaws on the small humorous bone in approval it proceeded to place the item firmly into a ditch.

It was a week to the day that the ambulance arrived at the sight. A doctor and two paramedics approached the concealed body that lay to the side of the excavations, with a blanket strewn casually across the still figure as a thickening pool of blood gathered in a ditch, offering a tasty meal to the stray that only a few days previously had enjoyed THAT bone. Removing the blanket for a moment the doctor turned away, his head leaning towards the blood filled ditch to be violently sick and immediately inviting the hungry dog to an even tastier meal.

His sickness was warranted; the man's face was without foundation, his skull shattered into a thousand pieces his eyes hanging by threads in an obtuse offering to their origin. Grey matter congealed about a for-head that offered little more than an extension to his shoulders, as the pressure of something unimaginable had diminished the skull into nothing less than a boned support for strips of blooded flesh.

"He'd been found at the bottom of the pit," a terrified workman exclaimed to the foreman in horror as he glanced at the mess. "He was winched up from the mud clutching a bone," he expanded in despair, adamantly refusing to return to the scene to see if any clues to his demise could be found.

A siren announced the arrival of the police as yet again Detective Chief Inspector Alan Lawson offered his interminable services to resolve, "this little problem," as he so elegantly put it, displaying little compassion or the offer of any sympathetic remark to the dead man's workmates as he went to view the body. He turned in disgust, retching persistently into THAT ditch his face white with eyes that sank slowly into sockets that he'd hoped would prevent him from seeing more. The dog looked at him in gratitude, wagging its tail in a show of appreciation to such a splendid feast as he tucked into a combined meal of both lunch and dinner. Returning to the body the Inspector instructed the paramedics to remove it from his sight. Life would not get any easier!

"It was obviously a very unfortunate accident," he acknowledged, more in hope than conviction as he took one more look at the skull. Again he was violently sick!

The usual enquiries ensued, with all present at the time of his death individually being interviewed.

"There were no witnesses! He was on his own! Having been drawn to a whimpering noise he'd heard from below, and, believing that perhaps it had been a cat or a dog he had clambered down to investigate further," appeared to be the common consensus, though no conclusions had been drawn.

"They had only discovered the body after hearing his terrified screams!" was something they all agreed on. "And whatever he'd seen or whatever had taken place down there they hadn't a clue, and neither did they want to know. They were leaving!"

The excavations ceased abruptly, leaving Arthur to decide that any further work to the mill's foundation might not be appropriate. With the introduction of a fresh team of workmen the pit was filled in and made good, with little to show for any intrusion on its sanctum but the sight of a single bone sticking grotesquely from the debris having been left by the more than satisfied dog.

Chapter IV

It was the day of the summer solstice, and after a dramatic storm the night before the sun reigned once again, displaying its dominance amongst the heavens as it kissed the Devon countryside with a new warmth that dispelled any belief that summer had come and gone in one day. The 'Druid Stone' stood tall and proud amongst the scrubland close to the mill-cottage, reminding all that this phallic to an age long gone symbolised the religious cults that had worshiped here over the centuries. Standing over fourteen feet in height and fifteen feet in circumference it offered servitude to those who chose to pay homage to the sun's power, its dying rays penetrated the six inch gap that split this granite monolith three feet down from its cragged head.

A celebration to its regard and mystical charm had been organised that evening, with a re enactment of the ancient ceremony of sun worship and sacrificial offerings to take place in fancy dress. Legend had it that chips of stone removed from the block had induced untold strength and virility to those who dared desecrate this holy shrine, resulting in extensive vandalism from the younger element in time immortal to put those theories to the test. Though tonight this requirement would not be needed, with alcohol offering an excellent substitute!

Preparations for the event and ensuing high jinks ran uninterrupted in the Martin family. The swimming pool offered more than just a place to swim and relax, but a place to conclude the initiation of those who had not participated before. This included Maria, Sonny, and poor Harry who insisted, "That the whole thing was just a childish venture for the gratification of those 'weirdoes' who delighted in delving in such superstitious rubbish."

"Not at all!" insisted an Amy whose recollection of the times spent when she as a young girl had revelled in drunken orgies of debauchery and lust around a stone that had offered nothing more that an excuse to do just that. And, who in wild abandonment to good taste had delighted in dress consisting of just garlands of freshly picked flowers and goodwill, her memories transporting her back to the joys of youth and enough to highlight the smile to a face that indicated that she was not beyond repeating such a venture.

"It was the one occasion in the year that allowed the village community complete freedom of expression," she announced convincingly, knowing only too well that this freedom often entailed dancing naked in a drunken stupor, and, with a raging hangover feeling very embarrassed the following morning.

First the village elders arrived, followed by the young men and women of a community that had certainly not lost its spirit and were only too eager to divulge their inhibitions in a night of revelry. A fire had been prepared close to the stone though well away from the mill, with fireworks, food, and plenty of drink for those who were - and who insisted they were - over the age of eighteen. Maria and Harry had soon got into the swing of things, with Harry's reservations fading into the slight breeze that cooled the warm evening air, turning his inhibitions into something slightly more than, "just a good time!"

Sonny for a change was without a male companion, seeking instead to enlist the company of Harry in a determined effort to succeed come what may. "It was now or never," she had queried calmly to herself encouragingly, as she persisted in her endeavour to secure his attention. Though without much success! Maria was sticking right by his side, with her memories of Tom's flirtation with her mother still strong in her mind.

The evening rolled on until the red-orange ball that had warmed their hearts throughout the day sank obligingly to the west and behind the stone, its rays penetrating the six- inch gap with intensity casting deep shadow across the field and on towards the cottage. It was now time for the initiations to commence as Maria, Sonny and Harry stood solemnly alongside three venturous young men who appeared game for anything, and, several highly motivated girls all keen to join into the swing of things; the girls each with their own very personal reasons but certainly mutual in one thing. The opportunity to get their hands on Harry!

A few late revellers had stayed on to watch, with a few more intent on making their mark. Children had been banned and the elderly had left. They had experienced the whole sordid affair on numerous occasions and it was now time for the young to fulfil their own fantasies. The sacrificial altar had been erected in front of the stone, with a partially frozen chicken impaled meticulously on a stake and positioned to one side in a liberal gesture to those animal lovers who would certainly object to any such sacrificial offering that might entail suffering to some living creature. Sonny was first to be offered to the 'Sun God' and ordered to remove her clothes down to her underwear, though without a thought she undressed completely.

"What in Gods name is going on now," muttered a confused Harry, his eyes focused on Sonny as willingly she conceded to any directive without thought or reservation, leaving her glazed eyes desperately trying to focus through a drunken haze on the proceeding. A garland of flowers was placed about her head the other around her neck as she was secured firmly to the altar, her breasts glistening in the heat of flames that licked eagerly to within feet of her, the sweat pouring in profusion about a body that had offered itself unequivocally to whatever was required of it as the horrified onlookers looked on.

"Something is wrong! This wasn't meant to happen, surely!" murmured a surprised Maria, as she followed the contours of a figure that now appeared detached from the sister she knew and loved, surrendering itself, "to what?" This was all new to them! Nothing like this had taken place before, with the experience of just good, honest, harmless fun throughout each and every previous sacrificial orientated ceremony overriding any suggestion that changes of a more insidious nature might be implemented. But now!

A large bowel filled with some obnoxious looking liquid was offered to the diminishing audience, leaving behind only those who took things seriously with the rest keen to take full advantage of the opportunity presented to them with that of, 'just a cheap thrill'! Each was instructed to consume a full goblet of the stuff, with Sonny forced to consume twice the amount. Not that it was required! Her mind had already been rendered obsolete.

Twenty minutes passed with each of the young villagers inspired to extract more than their fare share of the potion, leaving them excitable and disorientated as they cheered a burning chicken that had now taken on the effigy of some charred relic of the Devil incarnate.

The self proclaimed 'Grand Master'- dressed in a black hood, with a yellow and orange cloak that made little reference to anything that might depict anything, though might embarrass one into believing that here was nothing less than a configuration of splodges that appeared to have custard streaked across it, far less that of an effigy of the 'Sun God' - stood proudly, holding a burning torch in an enthused encouragement to the night spirits to sanction the initiation.

His voice echoed out in a loud and clear announcement decreeing that Sonny should remain at the altar for no less than fifteen minutes, during which time a male member of the flock - as he so patently put it, and a flock that now all appeared very drunk and indecisive - would have to consummate the initiation with intercourse. Sonny observed in silence! Nodding her head in approval as a young, blond, well muscled man ventured towards her in an enthusiastic response to the request for, a volunteer!

Pointing to a startled Maria the 'Grand Master' indicated that, "she would be next! If she still retained the courage to go through with it of course," he announced with conviction, his eyes piercing and intent, daring her to refuse. Her confused brain determined that the prospect of being called a coward was something that she was not prepared to allow, not wanting to let down those who had initiated the whole event, and, encouraged by Harry's increased enthusiasm to her participation. Peter had reservations, though he was very drunk! With David almost demanding that she go through with it!

The early departure of her parents and the fact that she was quite tipsy offered her reassurance. She agreed! "Though any consummation would have to be with Harry," she slurred, the effects of the alcohol and potion taking their toll. Further agreement was reached.

Sonny hung from the altar offering a mesmerised submission to her fate as the blond giant arrived to confront her, his nakedness expressing his desire not to let her or his encouragers down. The few stragglers that had stayed behind to feast on this erotica remained silent, focusing in awe as the giant's equally giant penis entered into the holy sacrament that had been bestowed on it, sinking within the confounds of Sonny's loins as her legs twitched in a heartfelt acknowledgement of its importance.

Her head reeled as the giant consumed her body in a passionate embrace, relinquishing any hold she may have had on self-restraint as she indulged in a moment of complete lust. Though restricted by her shackles! She had been well and truly consummated and had passed the initiation with flying colours, and with that, she fainted! The exuberance of the moment and that potion getting the better of her had instilled a moronic defiance to any morality she may once have acquired. A round of applause ensued, with the onlookers now directing their attention to Maria. David pushed her forward encouragingly, leaving her standing hesitantly in front of the 'Grand-Master', her thoughts responding to his directions in a hazed indication of her confusion.

"Must I?" she whispered to the man who was empowered to submit her body to, well…?   She knew!

"Must I?" she repeated, stuttering helplessly in an acknowledged acceptance that yes, she must.

"Yes!" He responded loudly. "It is now out of my hands, it has been passed over to 'The Great One', the only judicator within our sacred scrolls that has the authority to carry out such a task. Consider yourself lucky my dear," he smiled, offering her another drink of that strange cocktail that had been especially prepared for the occasion, and, which she readily accepted, having conceded to her fate as he proceeded to undress her.

Encouraged by the slow handclap and enthusiastic chanting she stepped towards the altar, her hands stretched in submission as she in turn was forcibly secured to the post, her feet drawn back inviting her legs to part as the slow hand claps and chanting increased to a crescendo. Drops of sweat sparkled in the bright light emitted from the glowing embers of a dying fire as she waited, her thoughts confused and searching as once again those memories of her childhood came flooding back.

"Why was she doing this? What ever possessed her to carry out such an absurd charade! After all that had happened to her in the…!" She held her breath! Then gasped, as her body trembled! Harry's penis had found its target as the agony and the ecstasy blended into one. For a moment there was total silence as the onlookers observed her changing mood. Closing her eyes with her fists clenched in a rigid demonstration of confused anger she raised her head to the stars, then, screamed! And screamed! Shouting! Shouting for him to stop!

"To fucking well stop and leave her alone! She'd had enough!"

The initiations were over, the party ceased to be a party as the stunned onlookers moved away, home to their thoughts and, their conscience. Harry untied Maria, carrying her still naked to the cottage as he tried to calm her, her hysterical screams lost in the cool misted air as they entered the security of a mill-cottage that offered her a place to come to terms with her own insecurity. Sonny passed her a dressing gown, insisting to Harry that she should now take over as leading her up the stairs and to her room she helped her into bed.

"The experience has all been too much," she sobbed to a concerned Sonny, who had little recollection of her own initiation! Which perhaps was for the best, having found herself lost to a situation best forgotten. They continued to talk, to exchange their thoughts and expectations in life as gradually Maria fell into. A very deep sleep!

Sonny smiled! "Now Harry would be hers for the taking," she mused in excitement, her speech still slurred as she congratulated herself on her initiative. He was still very tipsy and, the size of that penis! Wow! She couldn't wait!

Harry remained frustrated and embarrassed, having been made to look a complete idiot in front of all those people. He certainly had no reservations were Sonny was concerned. Her breasts had worked wonders on his imagination and, those thighs, the ones that could crush a wall-nut with one squeeze, he could already feel them tightening around his back. Sonny had returned to her room, her intentions fully confirmed her mind void from any other objective, her smile indicating that she was 'up to no good'. Arriving at the door she noticed Harry leaving Peter's room.

"Perfect!" she chuckled. "Action was required!"

"He would be spending the night there, but first he needed the bathroom, urgently!" Harry laughed as he bid her goodnight!

Sonny's room stood situated conveniently between Peter's room and the bathroom, offering her every chance to seduce Harry as he returned.

"Why not!" she smiled to herself, "after all, Maria had let him down and she was just, well, 'helping out a little'," she chuckled again. Leaving her bedroom door ajar and the light on she prepared for bed, offering herself for an innocent display of seduction as she ensured that as Harry passed the door he would reap the full benefits of each and every aspect of a body that was ready and waiting to be, 'thoroughly attended too'!

He certainly would as she stood naked in front of the mirror postulating in an unseeing pretence, resolutely to reach to the floor for a nightdress that bore little resemblance to anything other than an excuse. Harry stopped in his tracks, unable to draw himself away as standing to the side of the door he followed her movements with interest, his unwitting reflection encouraging Sonny to offer him more as she proceeded to indulge in her fantasies, watching his astonished face and noticing with excitement the increasing size of the bulge in his trousers. Her restraint was overcome with a desiring passion as her naked form moved speedily towards the door, giving him no chance of escape as her breasts confronted his embarrassment and almost suffocating him in the process.

"Please come in!" she remarked without reservation, "and make yourself comfortable while I slip into something, well, a little more comfortable," she smiled, her pretence at surprise and her efforts to cover herself both having an intentional 'lack of success' as her body sank within the folds of the duvet, her legs open and relaxed inviting further investigation.

Harry hesitated, his voice croaked and apologetic as he followed the contours of her body through the thinly spun fabric of a silken nightdress that allowed him to focus on a thick expanse of pubic hairs that seemed to glare invitingly from behind this translucent mantle. Drawing one knee to her chin her nightdress depleted before him, her thighs parting to expose the succulent delights that they protected as leaning back on the bed she invited him to join her.

He didn't hesitate, his erect penis extended to its full as it parted the orifice that remained moist and wanting; watching her face as she gasped in surrender to a monster that had found its new home. The ecstasy of the moment contorted her face as she groaned, "fuck me! Fuck me! Harder! Now!" she squealed, leaving the orifice that clung urgently to its prise unable to secure its length in full, with an increased acceptance that, "there was just too much of it!"

The door had closed tight as the faint glow from the night-light faded into the darkness. Neither of them noticed a thing, as consumed with passion Sonny lent towards a moon's shadow that cast nothing more that a dim reflection of her smile through the open window, offering Harry little but a glimpse of an inviting backside that had prepared itself for one soul purpose.

Again her whispered demands echoed eerily into the night sky as the passion of the moment took over. "Now!" she insisted in anticipation as arching her back Harry found the intended target, his fingers clinging to the fine strands of dark brown hair that stretched languidly across shoulders that remained tense, as pulling hard he forced her head back to contort and twist towards him. With a whimper, her eyes glazed in a smoulder of passion, she smothered his face with the fullness of lips softening to their touch. Immediately she drew back, horror now contorting her face, leaving her body to tremble her eyes to stare in an animated disbelief at what confronted her.

Spitting the blood from a mouth that once had been sensuous and consuming she tried desperately to draw away as Harry's head lolled across her shoulder in a limp surrender to his mortality, his lips distended in an obtuse reminder to their being as spouting a gurgling of gore and mucus his jaw remained dislocated and disjointed, exposing a throat that expounded to the depths of his stomach in a grotesque configuration to his demise. His face had been torn apart! Split asunder from a force unrivalled in its intensity by a creature or otherwise that offered no earthly substance as the formless shape blended into the shadows, leaving the room in a concerted reminder to its invincibility.

The wailing of a stricken fox, or was it a dog, echoed eerily from the direction of the adjoining mill as if to announce the death knoll of poor Harry, though making little inroads on the hysterical screams that now left Sonny's lips as she fled naked from her room.

Once again Detective Chief Inspector Alan Lawson arrived on the scene, only this time the tone of his voice indicated that a far more serious approach should be adopted, and one that differed completely to the occasion of his previous visit. The now well-rehearsed procedures were implemented, with the conclusion being that as in the first murder a similar situation had arisen, though with no further clues having been tendered.

"Apart from the discovery of that very same trail of clay and mud found in Maria's room that had now mysteriously found its way into Sonny's," the Inspector motioned resolutely.

"And, having transfixed itself to the thick, shag piled bedroom carpet, though its origin was still uncertain," he muttered cautiously to those in attendance.

"Another unsolved murder pending," sighed the Inspector, having arrived back at his office his determination to solve at least one of the murders inflicting nothing less than a pounding headache as he scrutinised every last item of documentation relating to the previous case, paralleling it with the present and coming up with. Absolutely nothing!

"This would not do his street credibility any good whatsoever," he sighed as he reflected on his now discredited nickname; a name known in the local constabulary by those who had admired his tenacity and fortitude in his endeavours to succeed as 'Sherlock-Lawson'. His reputation as a top sleuth had taken a dramatic tumble!

"Another unsolved murder," remarked the judge in an apologetic and sympathetic gesture of his frustration, offering once again an open verdict due to insubstantial evidence to a disgruntled and disconsolate gathering of Harry's relatives and friends.

Maria had followed the proceedings with intent, analysing every last detail her mind trying desperately to piece together a jigsaw that even the best investigative minds in the business had been unable to solve as she reflected on the death of the workman at the mill.

"All three deaths appeared to inter-relate around the presence of that earth and clay and, all three had sustained horrific injuries to their head," she acknowledged as she pursued her conviction with, "and something or someone seemed determined that any excavations associated with the strengthening of the mill's foundations or, that any interference by those who might be considered party to this either directly or indirectly, should pay the ultimate price," she voiced silently, remaining satisfied with her own reasoning!

"Though what sort of reasoning could possibly lay behind this spate of such vicious murders?" she concluded, leaving her to respond to her own questioning with a frustrated muttering of, "I haven't the slightest idea!"

Looking to God in the hope of some divine response to her analysis she found little more than an incomprehensive conclusion to her theory. "These bloody deaths remain a mystery, and who in hell will the next victim be?" she sighed dejectedly. Maria was in despair, her thoughts dwelling on what had taken place and having unwillingly to accept that the whole ugly business was nothing less than one horrific fact.

"Once again a member of her own family had - be it inadvertently - caused the death of yet another of her boyfriends. And! Once again they had been caught in a compromising situation with the same," she sobbed hopelessly.

"What the hell was going on!" she cried out loud. She had not believed her mother's version of accounts that, "she'd been raped!" On the contrary, she'd been inclined to believe that the reverse was more the operative. "She would never find true love," she acknowledged despondently, her eyes moistening as tears trickled slowly down cheeks that looked pale and drawn.

"And Sonny of all people!" she sobbed, feeling let down and rejected. "Her own sister and best friend," she mused in anger. "Who would be the next family member to hurt her? Would it be Peter? Surely not! Or David?" she muttered with venom in her voice. "Yes! He would be a certainty to inflict the wrath of God on her, if he got the chance!"

Sonny's apologies went unheard! The hurt had been achieved with a cold-hearted attempt to inflict maximum emotional damage to someone who had experienced enough of that in their short lifetime. Maria ignored her pleas for forgiveness with contempt, muttering that, "one day she would get her 'just deserts'," leaving Sonny to leave in a huff insisting that, "it was Harry who had taken advantage of her drunken state in any case," and, "that she had enjoyed every minute of it," smiling cynically. Maria again burst into tears, her anger swelling her determination to reap revenge now paramount in her thoughts.

Chapter V

Weeks then months past in a flotilla of resentment and unhappiness for Maria, her trust in the Martin family having taken a knocking with only Peter and her father showing any indication that they could be trusted. She refused to bring any of her friends, male or female home, concerned that they too could end up dead. What or who had offered asylum to the evil that had caused such misery still remained just as perplexing, and, she wasn't prepared to offer any of her friends as a human sacrifice to satisfy her understanding of such. She would wait!

The weather had changed dramatically from warm autumn sunshine to howling winds, merging into a northerly airflow bringing sleet and snow with a vengeance. Winter had entered into its usual conflict with nature's insistence that its animal and plant life should have equal success of survival, but! Not in these extremes.

Christmas would entertain the hardship of blocked roads and fallen power-lines and a covering of snow worthy of an Alpine ski resort. Though certainly not with the preparedness that accompanied it! The usual chaotic conditions prevailed throughout the West Country and the South East, offering little hope of an early release and, offering little hope of the Martin family venturing too far from their cottage. They would have to make the best of it!

Millrise cottage as usual was ready and prepared to meet the winter severities, with the old mill looking resplendent in the blanket of crisp white snow that shielded its aging structure from a frost that had sharpened its teeth in a determined effort not to be beaten, expanding and contracting the ancient timbers in an enthused attempt to determine whether the mill had a future or not. Standing up to the menace it offered a resilience that would have deterred almost any opposition to its being, remaining steadfast and firm and showing the world that 'The House that Jack built' would not be beaten.

Amy's attempt at ensuring that Christmas would be enjoyed met with glum looks from Maria and David, leaving Peter, Sonny and their parents to bring an element of cheer to an otherwise miserable day. The seasonal Christmas lunch would be held in the evening, at seven o'clock.

"And, enjoying themselves would be compulsory," insisted a perturbed Amy, "who after all was only trying to do what was for the best," she smiled nonchalantly, her best being to try desperately to put the past behind her and keep the family from drifting apart, though from all indications with little success!

"Well, that just wouldn't be enough!" retorted an angry Maria as she caught sight of Sonny cracking a joke at her expense, with of all people. David! "Uh!" she growled, her eyes blazing in his direction. "They could stick their stupid lunch," she exclaimed lividly, "right where they stuffed the turkey," she retorted, causing Sonny to break into a fit of uncontrollable laughter at the sight of her mother's astonished face. At that Maria decided that she had had enough as storming into the kitchen she poured herself a large whisky, to sit in the corner sobbing uncontrollably her thoughts and concentrations demanding that she didn't spend a moment longer than was necessary with her adopted family.

Time passed leaving the remainder of the family to continue with their meal, insisting that Maria would soon be hungry enough to rejoin them and that in any case sulking didn't come natural. Far from it! Maria had no intention of returning as she downed a further whisky, her mind retreating into a maze that lost her for a moment as she considered her position in the household.

The storm continued unabated, with the cold air seemingly finding every nook and cranny within the kitchen confounds, leaving a shivering Mara to finally decide that the radiator's thermostat should be adjusted as her stay in the kitchen would be a long one.

Any merrymaking within the family gathering had ceased to be, leaving an increasingly intoxicated David deciding to excuse himself from the table as, "he required time to think, and the bedroom provided the only place where he could gather his thoughts," he muttered, leaving the depleted family gathering acknowledging his strange observations with a shrug and mutual in their soundings that it was, "David just being David!"

But David had no intentions of going to his room; his thoughts were elsewhere as he tapped on the kitchen door. The door remained unlocked, and without awaiting a reply he sauntered in to confront a Maria that had now consumed her fourth glass of whisky. David approached cautiously, offering her a consoling arm and wishing her no harm.

For a moment she held back, feeling his breath on the nape of her neck the stench of alcohol disgusting her. He spoke reassuringly, condemning Sonny and their mother for making a fool of her and insisting that as a brother he could offer her a different kind of love. Maria's suspicions rose, and although slightly tipsy she could easily tell when David was lying. On this occasion her suspicions were well founded as she held her ground, her eyes darting in every direction as urgently she sought protection, some defensive means of repelling any sudden undesirable, unwarranted burst of anger or uncontrolled lust. The look in his eyes terrified her!

"Reassuring words and a calm though assertive response should do the trick," she acknowledged as carefully she went to remove his arm, but with little success. In a marked contradiction to her wishes his arm drew tighter, with his fingers placed firmly around her shoulders his left hand reaching for the lock on the door as he forced her towards the kitchen table. His voice changed! Aggressive then sympathetic, commanding then suggesting, offering concerned gestures of understanding to her fears as quietly he reached for a knife.

"Why are you doing this?" whispered a terrified Maria. "I thought you were fond of me?" she queried as she tried to scream, but was immediately silenced by a dishcloth that was pushed violently into her mouth, leaving her eyes begging to be released as the point of the knife played threateningly across her neck.

"Undress!" he ordered pulling impatiently at her dress, ripping her bra from breasts that heaved in a terrifying acknowledgement to their fate to immediately feel threatened with instant death if she refused to adhere to his demands.

"Now bloody well do as I say!" he commanded in a drunken drawl as he pushed the petrified Maria back across the table, his eyes crazed and dilated with lust and a good deal of alcohol as he studied his prey. With the knife still at her throat he released the belt supporting his trousers, letting them fall freely to his ankles fully satisfied that his performance would not be impeded as dropping his pants he forced her legs apart impatiently.

Offering no resistance Maria stared impassively as his expression took on a more serious approach, knowing that to show emotion of any kind would only encourage him to pursue something terminal against her.

"He could not rape her and allow her to live, allow her to tell all and destroy him," she queried despondently. "He would rape and then kill her. She would wait! Wait for any opportunity to strike back, strike before the inevitable took place."

Her body tingled as his erect penis pressed hard against her thigh, his face contorting into an idiotic grin as gripping her thighs he pulled her towards him in an eagerness to pursue his conviction. She remained still, allowing her body to submit to his demands as the knife was pressed forcefully into her throat, her thoughts twisting and turning as if lost in some scrambled nightmarish horror that found her sinking into a dark abyss where soon her life would be taken from her in one merciless and hideous way. She now remained fully convinced that he would kill her, even if she dare so much as move an inch as her eyes followed his penis in disgust.

Her fingers tightened as she sensed that soon, very soon, 'that thing' would achieve its objective. "And then what!" The memories flooded back, first of her father and those disgusting 'things' he did to her, then to those horrible girls who delighted in teasing her with their interminable list of obscenities, forcing her into positions that had her convinced she would break every bone in her body as they subjected her to a stream of abuse. For a moment her thoughts were lost to these miseries she had endured as her eyes moistened. And then there was that care officer she had turned too for help.

"Why had he been such a bastard to her when she had accepted that her life wouldn't change and that he could do what the fuck he wished with her," she motioned furiously, the tears trickling down her cheeks at the recollection of such horrors.

"Why, inwardly she had been soulless and dead anyway, with her resilience to withstand such endless suffering having crumbled completely, so what did it matter!" she mused as the reality of her predicament left her for a moment.

Closing her eyes she waited, waited for that 'thing' to enter into a sordid communion with her body as tensing her legs and arching her back she prepared at least to ensure that the pain would be bearable. The 'thing' reached the optimal position before entry, only to be quickly withdrawn as a knock at the door heralded the arrival of Peter, asking her, "if she was OK as the door was locked," and, "had she seen David?" Her relief was clear! Her hero had arrived to save her from this insidious bastard.

"Peter! Her dear Peter would rescue her from the jaws of hell; her knight in shining armour had come to claim his prize and smite dead the evil creature that soon was to breathe fire on her soul and destroy her."

But her fantasising served little in offering her freedom - or anything near as such - as she held her breath. In one frantic bid she twisted her head to face the door, trying desperately to scream but it was no use, she could feel the point of the knife embedding itself in her neck, leaving her with little choice but to remain silent. The removal of the cloth came next as Peter insisted that, "she respond, or he'd be left with no other choice than to force open the door."

The knife sank further, demanding that she reply, drawing blood as she croaked out loud that, "she was being sick," and, "to leave her alone."

Remaining unconvinced Peter pushed at the door, offering her help if only she would, "open the bloody thing and let her in."

For a moment David's eyes averted as he focused on a chair, reaching towards it with urgency convinced that to jam it under the door handle would restrict any possibility of entry. Maria took her chance! Lifting her foot she caught him resoundingly in the groin, knocking him back gasping as he tripped over his trousers, banging his head against the wall with a resounding thud the knife staring at her in a horrific reminder of what it stood for. David's demise! He had pushed his knifed hand against the wall to cushion the fall, twisting his wrist in the process with the point of the knife sinking deep into his abdomen.

"There was no question about it," she muttered excitedly as she followed his movements, her smile saying it all as slowly he sank to the floor. Almost in an acceptance that the outcome proportioned the crime she crept towards him, her nakedness reminding her what an insidious bastard he'd been as she felt for a pulse. There was none! "He was dead all right!"

Peter continued with his knocking, reminding her that, "both kitchen doors were locked," and, "what was that noise and what in hell's name was she playing at?"

"She couldn't let him in! There was no knowing what he might do. She had to allay his fears, convince him that she was indeed being sick, somehow!" For a moment she allowed herself the satisfaction of staring at the body, feeling no emotion and glad that this creature had finally succumbed to his atonement with the Devil. "He would be a long time dead!" she smiled again, though still numbed and in shocked submission to his actions.

Covering the body with the tablecloth and scattering a number of plates and cups across the whole area she shouted that, "she was coming," and, "that he could see for himself that she was being sick, that's if he didn't fucking well believe her!" she muttered.

Drenching her hair and squeezing mayonnaise mixed with pickle across the front of what remained of a dress ripped and torn she smeared it in thoroughly, holding it across her arm to her front along with her bra as she unlocked the door.

Peter's face dropped, several inches as he stared in amazement at the hardly concealed figure of his sister peering almost naked from behind the door, her clothes excreting a horrible vomit like substance that certainly convinced him that she was telling the truth. Wafting them to his face forgetting that she was still in a state of undress she demanded that, "he leave her to be sick in peace," and, "that she was feeling fucking terrible!"

For a moment his eyes focused on her breasts, his thoughts hovering on the brink of a world that forbid him to enter further, his brotherly love for a sister that remained just that dispensing thoughts that could easily be mistaken for wishful thinking as his eyes quickly diverted from a body that offered more than just a glimpse from behind the loose ends of a dress that – although innocent to him - had been torn from her person. This proved enough to convince him that here was territory that was defiantly taboo as apologising in whispered embarrassment he left her to her sickness.

She felt sick, though sick of a different sort, sick at what she had done and hating herself for having taken such critical measures against her darling brother.

"But what choice did she have! What else could she possibly do to convince him to leave her alone, and, with a body that somehow had to be removed, and on her own!" For a brief moment she allowed herself a smile, realising that her diverter tactics had paid off, having unwittingly been achieved with an almost masochistic display of calculation and purpose.

"My darling Peter," she sighed. "Marry me!" She wished!

It was time to think, think very hard her head still throbbing both from her terrifying ordeal and the effects of the whisky.

"First she would require fresh clothes. Ah! In the laundry basket just the thing, a pair of jeans that Sonny had worn only yesterday. She would drown in them," she acknowledged with a smile as she reached for a warm jumper that too belonged to Sonny. "And that!" she confirmed as the white woollen garment hung like a bell-tent across a figure smaller by three sizes at least. No bra, no pants but, a pair of Peter's underpants would suffice.

"Perfect!" she laughed, feeling her crutch tingle at the thought of what delights they had comforted. "One day!" She sighed again, "one day!"

"What to do with the body! Soon the kitchen would be required, and then what? Perhaps to offer a more rational reason for remaining in the kitchen would give her the opportunity to sort something out and allay the inevitable! She had to convince her family of something," she pondered solemnly. Opening the door a little she announced that, "she was going to surprise them all with one of her specialities, a delightful sherry trifle!" "Convincing!" she questioned. "Well! She could live in hope!"

She could hear mutterings of approval as she indicated that, "she would be at least forty minutes," and, "not to come in!" Again further mutterings resounded from the within the dinning room as an agreement was reached.

"That would be fine!" her mother declared apprehensively, still undecided as to Maria's real condition after the way in which she left the table.

"Now she could think clearly," Maria mused as she surveyed the mess. "How the hell could she transport the body, and to where?" she groaned, "he must weigh a good fifteen stone and it was still snowing heavily." She needed an answer, and quickly! "The old mineshaft would be an obvious choice, but that was a good hundred yards away and at least seventy from the furthest point to the mill. But! She had little choice, she would have to, 'go for it'!" she decided apprehensively.

"First she must remove the knife, replace it with perhaps a sharp stone to make it appear like at accident, indicate that it had embedded itself within him as he fell into that three hundred foot chamber of horrors that would remain his grave, hopefully!" she grimaced. "Why, he wouldn't be the first to lose their way and end up in that watery mineshaft, a mineshaft where escape would prove impossible - even if anyone had miraculously survived the fall - and that now would be thick with mud and slime," she shivered at the thought. "And nor would he be the last!" she decided acceptingly. She couldn't understand why it hadn't been closed off to the public ages ago. "Still, that was fine by her!"

"First to find a wheelbarrow!" as deciding to rap up with two further jumpers and a bright tartan scarf belonging to her mother, found in the wash basket alongside some woolly leggings and the tea-cosy that supplemented for a bonnet and fitted perfectly, she pulled out a pair of Wellington boots belonging to Peter that almost covered her thighs. At last she was ready, and without caring how she looked or who the hell each of the items belonged too she ventured out into the night and the storm, heading towards the potting shed as best she could.

The icy blast almost bowled her over as she struggled through the thick blanket of snow, arriving at the shed her optimism lost in the swirl of the storm as she reached for the door.   The wheelbarrow stood to one corner covered in rags and dust, with her fortunes continuing having found a lamp still containing oil with a wick that had seen better days though no torch. Even so, both offered some hope as she prepared to return back to the cottage, with five minutes having already past as she ploughed her way through the knee-high drifts almost in tears.

"What chance did she have of going anywhere it such conditions and, with a fifteen stone load," she sobbed, as reaching the kitchen door she found. Nothing! The body had gone! Just a thin trail of earth and clay stretching from the door towards the area where the body had lay, and all that remained of David's presence and his death as she returned to the open door. She looked in astonishment and dismay at the empty wilderness lying before her, trying desperately to focus through the driving snow as to her left there appeared a rapidly diminishing serration of what obviously had been that of some heavy load. The trail lead convincingly in the direction of the mill's boundaries, in a strait line and on towards the shaft as it disappeared into the gloom.

"Someone has moved it," she gasped, her head swirling her eyes demanding that this illusion recant to render itself a reality. It was not to be, with the broken snow offering little indication as to what or who had willingly come to her rescue. There were no footprints!

Few options remained! She would have to follow the trail, to find out what the hell was going on and who in God's name was helping her. But first! First she must ensure that if her family were to discover her absence then to determine a search party would be without question. If that was to take place then heaven knows what they might find.

Opening the door her voice once again reached out to the dinning room, announcing sheepishly that, "she had again been sick! Only this time all over the sherry trifle!" Groans and further mutterings ensued followed by Peter's voice calling hesitantly, "are you sure you don't require help?"

She assured him that, "she didn't thank you very much," smiling at the courage it must have taken to ask as her thoughts dwelt back to his shocked expression as he'd surveyed her near nakedness just a short time earlier.

"She would still make the trifle," she insisted, "although it could take slightly longer as she'd have to get some fresh ingredients from the Richards next door," she persisted. "They wouldn't mind, and the snow had eased a little," she lied. It certainly hadn't!

Maria's worried parents offered a chorus of initial concerns, though quickly dispelled by Maria who insisted that the fresh air would do her good. "Get rid of the sickness and the bloody hangover," she shouted back, "and, give me time to get my head together," she laughed, hoping to convince them that she'd forgiven her mother and Sonny although that was something that she certainly didn't intend doing.

First, ensuring that no trace of David's presence remained in the kitchen and that she remained fully protected from the elements she lit the oil lamp, and having donned her heavy jacket, scarf and boots thus ensuring she wouldn't freeze, looking like a mummified Yeti she prepared to leave.

"I won't be long," she shouted as once again she ventured out into the wilderness, following the now rapidly deteriorating trail as she headed towards the shaft, her thoughts fearful of what she could encounter but determined to see it through.

The night air offered nothing but a frozen spectrum of iced formations hanging languidly from branches and twigs, endeavouring to hinder her progress and her spirit in a seemingly endless mystical fantasy that confronted her. The night sky reflected little from a waning moon, though offering just enough to sustain her on her way, with this unrelenting struggle through the storm only succeeding in highlighting a continued respect to its remorseless ferocity and enough to convince her that whoever or whatever it was dragging that body through this cascading response to a spiritual antinomy, must have the strength of five men!

"Who or what-else could achieve such strength," she gasped in an un-daunting acknowledgement to this phenomena's achievement, having now remained fully convinced that it offered nothing less than some ethereal reincarnation willing to assist her in her time of need.

"It was certainly not of this world!" she gasped again in exhaustion. There remained no footprints, the body had been hauled unceremoniously through thick gorse, across ditches, and had even snapped the occasional thicker of the branches from the many saplings that had not long been planted to assist in an ailing woodland.

"A guardian Spirit!" she smiled, "a guardian Spirit is watching over me!" she panted, her legs weakening with each stride. "Another thirty yards and I'll be there," she muttered, recognising the enormous grey-black trunk of the resident oak guarding the entrance to the shaft in a stance of military exactitude to its authority just ten feet from the entrance, its ominous and inhospitable form offering a stark reminder to anyone foolish enough to approach too closely that to step any nearer could result in their tripping on one of its large winding roots, causing one to disappear within an instance down the mineshaft to a certain death.

Within fifteen to twenty minutes of exhaustive battling against the elements she arrived at the mine-shaft to find David's body lying sprawled at the edge, his face and hands covered in scratches and dirt his clothes ripped and blooded. Falling to her knees thoroughly worn out she stared soulfully at the body!

"Something was wrong," she pondered, focusing on the trail leading back to the mill-cottage. "Surely there would have been some trace of blood left by the body, some obvious sign that if anything it had indeed been dragged along that trail," she reflected! There was none, leaving Maria to wonder in horrified silence!

Clambering to her feet she scoured the area for any interference. There was none! It was as if she'd travelled miles, miles of exhaustive trekking through the storm but still she remained just a short distance from the mill, although its adjacency to the far right of the mill-cottage seemed like an eternity. The wind still howled as the icy flakes spat at her in a sporadic desire to torment her skin, distorting her vision though not distracting from her certainty that she could hear faint noises echoing soulfully through the storm's ceaseless ferocity.

"Whimpering or sobbing," she deduced in a muttered appraisal to her reckonings, "coming from the direction of the mill's base," was her final construed but unsure soundings as her ears strained to audit her suspicions.

"It could be conceivable that perhaps the storm was playing tricks with her hearing," she accepted, her eyes trying desperately to focus through the blinding snow, eventually to pick out the familiar outline of, 'The house that Jack built', as her father so affectionately called it. It looked an ominous sight in the darkness, looming towards her in its mantle of snow its size distorted by this white shroud that offered up some ghostly apparition as it sat solitary within its surrounds. The mill's wheel offered more than being 'just a wheel', its position alongside the mill-wall depicting its historical splendour and enhanced by a support of jewel daggered icicles lying host in the arches and slats that now stood dormant. The stream had frozen solid, its icy grip ensnaring the wheel in a manacled desire to torment. Though the 'Sun God' might consider such arrogance with distain!

"Strange!" Muttered Maria poignantly, "Why do I feel that I've been here before, that in some way I've always lived there?" she acknowledged silently. Turning slowly she took another look at the body, focusing in shocked silence as to her front she could pick out those very same dustings of clay and earth that were present at the scene of each murder.

"It was as though this somebody or something had a vested interest in ensuring that she should remain safe, and single! But why?" she asked herself yet again. But, there was no time to stand and ponder on such a theory; time was running out, she must get back before her parents became suspicious.

A sharp jagged stone lay conveniently at hand and partly concealed in snow as scraping away the thin layer she took hold of a heavier rock. Placing the point of the stone over the gash - inflicted earlier by the knife to David's abdomen - she stood ready, her agonised mind allowing her little sentiment.

"Now!" she whispered hesitantly, raising the rock as she held her breath. But still her turmoil mind was crying out, screaming at her, reminding her that. "She was innocent! She didn't kill him! He killed himself! HE tried to rape her!" she cried aloud as, slam! The rock hit the stone with a resounding thud, sending it deep into David's abdomen, splitting the skin and disembowelling him such was the force. Maria retched violently, her eyes staring in disbelief at what she had just done as wrenching at the body she rolled it to its side in a frantic bid to complete the job; a job neither pleasant nor gratifying but a job well done and all that was required.

Staring emphatically at the deep void that seemed only too eager to offer up its eternal soul to any awaiting client that might seek sanctuary within its confounds she pushed remorselessly at David's unrelenting form, following it with a satisfied smile as it disappeared three hundred feet down a mineshaft that now presented itself as an epitaph to his mortality. A body now lost to the rats and maggots whose gastronomic juices would savour the memory of such a splendid Christmas feast for years to come. Her smile of satisfaction said it all. "He would never bother her again!"

Clearing the mess and depositing it down the shaft she was quick to ensure that nothing was left to chance, and, that nothing could attract attention. The blooded snow surrounding the hole had been removed, along with all the gory bits as kicking a layer of fresh snow over the whole area she now felt convinced that there was nothing that could offer even the slightest indication that she, or anyone else for that matter had been there. Resting for a second she attempted to gather her wits, shivering as the swirling snow continued in its relentless task to extract the most out of her tired body. And! As for the clay and earth! "So what," she mused! "She didn't leave it there, but who did!" she questioned herself again.

Deciding that she must at least show her face at the Richards or suspicion might be aroused she retraced her steps, following carefully the faint outline left by the body, "or was it a log, or some dead animal perhaps, and, did it really matter? No!" she concluded as she continued in making her way cautiously alongside her own tracks, veering off heading towards their house and arriving at the doorstep exhausted.

An astounded Mrs Richards responded to her knock with enthused concern, astonished that a young girl should be wondering about in the dark, "and in such weather," she scolded, - "and sounding just like her mother," were Maria's immediate thoughts, - "and on her own," Mrs Richards continued unrelenting, as she glanced behind Maria just to ensure there was no other foolhardy person lurking in the shadows.

"Not only sounding like her mother, but now a combination that included both Sonny and Peter," Maria smiled inwardly.

Accepting Mrs Richards's concern with gratitude Maria countered by politely explaining that, "she had fallen on the icy surface en route, which accounted for her condition," and, "had they such a thing as 'trifle mix' and a number of the ingredients required that would ensure that the preparation of, "a trifle good enough to surprise her family as she was hopeless at cooking, or preparing anything for that matter!." Again she smiled inwardly, having realised that she must sound like some bloody idiot rattling on about trifle-mix in the middle of a blizzard, though completely unconcerned as the response Mrs Richards offered indicated just that, with a, "what the hell was she wondering around in a storm searching for trifle-mix, was she mad!" though dictated with a rather yielding approach.

Her eagerness to make amends on seeing the forlorn look on Maria's face was indicated with a, "Well, you might just be in luck!" as she continued to respond in an increasingly inspired zeal that, "They had!" To which Maria was eagerly invited to step inside and warm herself. Which she did! Willingly!

The burning embers threw off an inviting glow as she stood before the fire, having removed the top two layers of clothing as warming her hands and legs her memories of events slipped away, leaving her to sip gratefully at a large glass of brandy with Mr Richards insisting that, "it was just the thing to warm her up on such a cold night!"

"It certainly was," she muttered, "and more!"

Roger - the elder of the three Richard's children - who at the age of eighteen had over the past three years admired Maria from a distance, suggested that perhaps a hot shower would do the job more effectively, perhaps allaying any possibility of catching a cold or worse, the flue.

"He certainly lives in hope, "she smiled knowingly to herself, with his offer to assist declined with gratitude. She recognised within an instance exactly what he had in mind!

"Anyhow, I must get back," she insisted. "I'll soak in a nice hot bath when I get home," she emphasised, "naked!" she whispered in the ear of an embarrassed Roger, whose face flushed as he fantasised her delightful form reclining in the bath in full view of. Him! And! Inviting him to join her as her breasts heaved in anticipation of his touch.

His fantasy was interrupted with a whispered, "Goodnight!" from Maria, as rubbing the objects of his desire casually against him she reached for the door remarking, "and pleasant dreams," as with a sigh a wink and a wiggle of her hips once again she advanced into the stormy surrounds that did little to enthuse her return home. She would have been quite happy having that shower with or without Roger's observations through the bathroom keyhole. She wasn't stupid!

Her arrival home damp and cold and with this time having actually succeeded in falling in the snow was met by her concerned parents as she let herself in through the kitchen backdoor. Announcing that, "she was home," and, "with the trifle-mix," her declaration was dismissed by a distressed father who immediately enquired, "had she seen David on her travels, he was missing?"

Her heart skipped a beat as she announced that, "she hadn't!" insisting that, "perhaps he was in the garage, or had gone for a walk. If only they knew," she smiled secretively, "knew that the horrible bastard was dead!" she muttered unconcerned.

"He wasn't anywhere to be found in the house," he continued, "and, he has been feeling very low," he reminded her.

"He was certainly that!" she smirked, her concentrations now directed at the bemused household cat as her father left to continue his search. "At least three hundred foot low," she exclaimed to a perplexed Tiddles, who was left with little choice but to agree as she purred for her supper.

Showing slightly more concern Maria offered to return to the Richards, "to ask if they had seen him as the power lines were still down and their mobiles weren't picking up a signal," she emphasised, "though thankfully their generator still supplied enough power for their needs," she continued thoughtfully, while remaining totally indifferent as to what their bloody generator was doing. "It could blow up as far as she was concerned," she mumbled dispassionately to herself.

Her offer to help was gratefully accepted, "as Peter had gone to the Johnson's and Sonny the Petersons, and then on to the village police station if they had no luck," motioned her troubled father, having accepted Maria's offer with relief.

Maria swallowed hard, insisting that, "he was sure to be somewhere," but unable to resist with a muttered, "though not at the bottom of a mineshaft," as she prepared to leave.

Arriving once again at the Richards she was invited in by an excitable Roger, who remained convinced that the wink, and that wiggle had been an open invitation to expound on his own theory of relativity; with all things being equal and that therefore his own feelings should be comparable to Maria's. Some chance!

Explaining the problem she was assured that David had been nowhere near the house, though the offer of that shower was still open, "if she remained convinced that he probably had gone to the village church for some spiritual enlightenment that was," smiled the obliging Mrs Richards, keen to see that the poor girl had the opportunity to relax and warm herself, or otherwise!

"She certainly remained convinced," Maria assured the smiling Mrs Richards as again she winked at the increasingly alert Roger, who was already devising a way in which he could explore to its maximum the opportunity to surrender his soul, and his luck, and avail himself of that hole in the bathroom wall that still hadn't been filled.

"The bathroom stood to the left of the small bedroom," instructed an increasingly smiling and enthused Mrs Richards, whose own relationship with her husband had ground to a halt almost a year ago, and who's newly discovered sexual liberation allowed her to deviate from time to time.

"She would bring up some towels when she was settled," she promised the unwitting Maria, "and to leave the door unlocked so that she wouldn't disturb her," she called as Maria followed her instruction.

As promised Mrs Richards arrived with the towels, placing them on the rail to the side of the bath as she chatted excitedly to a naked and unenthused Maria, who continued with her ablutions unperturbed.

"Strangely enough she had intended to take a shower herself," she informed the totally unconcerned Maria, who insisted that, "she should go ahead unless it was the bath she required? And if that was the case she could easily swap!"

Showing encouragement at her lack of concern Mrs Richards acknowledged that, "perhaps the door should be closed, just in case!" her voice now oblivious to the increasingly bored and weary Maria, who by now was beginning to draw her own conclusions on Mrs Richards and couldn't give a fuck what in God's name she did, she just wanted to bathe.

Mrs Richards proceeded to undress, her forty one year old figure doing her credit as she turned on the shower, insisting that Maria must have run all the hot water and that with their generator at its maximum the water still only remained tepid.

"Well would you care to join me?" motioned the hapless Maria with a sigh, keen to oblige with almost anything just to keep this damn woman quiet. "The bath is certainly large enough," she grimaced as the grateful Mrs Richards squeezed excitedly between Maria and the rubber duck, a duck that had just seen its fortunes extinguished at a stroke its deliverance to eternal damnation sealed forever as Mrs Richard's ample bottom squashed it to 'Kingdom-come'.

She continued to chat as Roger observed the proceedings through 'that hole', astonished to see his own mother massaging Maria's shoulders, naked, and in the bath. His eyes deepened into distant pools of light as they swallowed whole the images of his mother, her hands moving unrestrained down towards Maria's breasts, asking, "if she was bothered," and, "that she had been fully trained in a variation of 'alternative massaging treatments' of which this was one."

Roger spluttered and Maria sighed again, smiling as she informed Mrs Richards that, "she could do what the fuck she liked, she was beyond caring," as she relaxed in the warm water. Mrs Richards took this as an indication that she could do 'exactly that' as her hand worked slowly across her abdomen, reaching down towards her loins as Roger focused in astonishment and disbelief at his mother's impudence.

"She was a lesbian!" he acknowledged in an exalted acclamation of his own understanding. "They both were," he gasped as he watched Maria stretching back to enjoy his mother's attentions, eventually to surface and embrace, standing in naked innocence and innocuous to Roger's observations as they towelled each other down, leaving his mind in turmoil his trousers damp as again he followed the contours of his mother in disbelief.

His inability to detach himself from his observations were reflective in his desire to see more, finding himself unable to resist the impulse to admire the full and firm breasts that offered their charm and desire in doing justice to hips that had bourn three children, of which he had been one. Expounding onto a firm abdomen that entertained the first signs of a thick bush of pubic hairs there bore little evidence that the women that had brought him into this world had diminished in her sexual desirability. But he had seen enough as he moved away. "He would now see his mother in a different light. And, as for Maria! Wow!"

Both returned to the lounge area as Mrs Richards offered a whispered thanks to Maria for entertaining her, insisting that, "she must come again, anytime!"

Replying that, "she would love to," Maria thanked them all for their concern over David, at the same time inviting Roger, "to join her sometime, to watch a DVD or something. She was often lonely!" though with no real desire that any undertaking would ensue.

Roger jumped at such an opportunity. "Lesbian or not he could certainly fuck her. If she was willing of course," he smiled to himself excitedly. Though with no chance!

Returning home the house remained calm. Her parents had taken the Land-Rover heading for the village in the hope that they might spot David, and as for Peter and Sonny, they were still out searching.

"David couldn't have driven his car even if he'd wanted," her father had insisted as he'd organised the search party. "In these conditions the only vehicle standing any real chance of making it would be a 4x4," he'd indicated as he'd prepared exactly that.

The rest of the party had gone on foot, which of course had at the time included Maria, but now there was just her at home, and she had a plan!

"Why not arrange it so that it bore all the hallmarks of a suicide attempt," she pondered in amused silence. "She would use his laptop to write a note and leave it in his draw, the police would find it later, and, if and when the body was found, voila! What could be simpler," she chuckled!

Ensuring the coast was clear she headed for his bedroom. First she put on a pair of thin surgical gloves found in the medical cabinet to ensure that fingerprints wouldn't be left, then, switching on the laptop and using battery power she proceeded to write the suicide note:

To my dear family!

For more than three years now I have developed an obsession for my dear sister Maria.
This has become more than just a fetish or infatuation; it has succeeded in taking over my whole life.
I think of her all the time and dream about her at night.
I see her smile in the sunshine, her tears in the raindrops, and see her body in the heavenly clusters of stars that form our universe.
Once in the spirit world we will be together, I know it in my heart! But until then, I have reached a point in time were knowing that we can never be together in this life has proved to be unbearable.
I have therefore decided to take my life.
I love you all, and especially you Maria, and I know that we will all meet up once again.
God be with you.

David Martin.

⇥⇤

Maria scanned the letter in satisfaction. "Perhaps slightly over the top," she smirked, "but that should certainly do the trick," she smiled confidently. "They'll certainly think he finally lost it completely after reading that," she laughed out loud. Printing out the letter courtesy of electricity from the generator carefully she forged his signature, remembering to use her left hand as he had. Next she opened the bottom drawer, her face changing from one whose composure had stabilised to that of anger and disbelief as for a moment she sat in shocked silence.

"The dirty bastard," she cried! "That fucking dirty bastard," she cried again as she held a photo of herself standing in the shower soaping herself down. She found more! The one of Harry making love to her in her bedroom, "it's a close up of me," she gasped in horror, "and doing…!" she couldn't bring herself to say the words. She felt sick!

She had seen enough as she placed the suicide note between the piles of photos that had been carefully positioned under his clothes. "Surely now they'll remain fully convinced that his obsession had far and away exceeded the realms of any reasonably sane person," she grimaced. "He was a bloody pervert!"

The sound of a car engine heralded the return of her parents as they pulled up beneath the lounge window, giving her just enough time to remove herself from David's room with 'that' photo of herself sunbathing in the garden still held firmly in her hand. Heading for her bedroom she placed "that bloody obscenity" in her own draw with a snarl. "Dirty bastard!" she remarked once again, "dirty bastard!"

The front door slamming shut was followed by her father shouting if anyone was at home. Maria ran down the stairs to greet them. "The Richards hadn't seen him nor had the Collins next door to them," she informed him with a renewed burst of enthusiasm that helped distract her from, "the bloody photos!"

"Well, the police have been informed and they'll be over as soon as the storm has abated," he retorted with concern. "They are very busy as you might expect!"

Sonny's arrival was not quite as peaceful as opening the door she again tripped over the cat, landing headfirst in that very same trifle that Maria had forgotten about in the rush. Clawing at the dripping mess of custard and cream that seemed to have delighted in sticking to her neck and shoulders she ran up the stairs to shower, shouting that, "there's been no sign of David by anyone and, I'm bloody freezing! And now covered in cream and custard," she laughed!

Peter was only moments behind Sonny as letting himself in he too immediately slipped on the remnants of the trifle, his face, hands and clothes covered in the stuff as he followed his sister's footsteps to clamber up the stairs, also shouting that, "he needed a good shower," and, "that David hadn't been seen by anyone. Though Sonny might have some news when she arrives back," he shouted once again, having concluded his announcement before anyone could inform him that she had in fact already arrived back as he charged into the bathroom to shower.

The noise as the bathroom door slammed shut startled poor Sonny into turning the shower off immediately as standing to the corner her breathing increased, with her chest tightening not daring to move an inch as she held her breath, listening in fear as the intruder moved about.

"Please God help me," she whispered to her divine master, "I'm too young to die!" she insisted, her eyes closed her lips motioning for some form of saving grace to her plight.

Oblivious to his sister's fears and locking the door behind him Peter decided that perhaps a bath might be more soothing, though with just the generator to warm the water to gage the temperature would be impossible. Undressing quickly and completely unaware of Sonny's presence he ran the water. Sonny held her breath!

"Perhaps her parents lay dead in a heap on the floor, mutilated beyond belief having succumbed to some horrific attack," she mused in horror, "and now this madman was washing the blood from his person readying himself for his next victim," she gasped. "She would be next!" she stuttered her eyes moistening as she crouched in terror awaiting her fate, preying again for some divine intervention, and then!

"She must defend herself!" she grimaced as picking up the shower brush and grasping it hard in her right hand she peered from between the curtains to see Peter's back and bottom as he proceeded to douse himself down. "I'll get the bastard before he gets me," she stuttered fearfully, as creeping slowly towards him in a naked abandonment to her fears with the shower brush raised menacingly above her she brought it down sharply on the back of his head, watching him sink into the bathwater half submerged in a stunned bewilderment.

Peter remained dazed as desperately he tried to fend of the mad creature that had insisted on attacking him in a frantic bid to do him harm or worse, a mad creature who had resorted to screaming hysterically, with her arm about his neck reigning what seemed to be a brush down at him from all angles, leaving her breasts to press hard into his back as struggling he tried desperately to gain the initiative.

The initiative was finally succeeded as reaching back his hands gripped hard at the flaying strands of Sonny's hair waving in abandonment as the melee continued. Pulling her forwards his strength superseding her determination as dragging her head hard across his shoulders he forced her body firmly against his back. For a moment they remained suspended in a mutual and exhaustive embrace, then slipping on the soap they collapsed into the bath water in a frenzied display of congeniality as their eyes met in recognition of each other.

"You fool!" she laughed, "you great big fucking fool!" she laughed again, more in relief than anything else as giving him one big hug her fears subsided, explaining that, "she'd been in the shower and had thought he was an intruder, or worse, a murderer!" Laughing they stood back, admiring each others physique in a platonic display of brother/sisterly affection as quickly drying themselves they returned to be greeted by their concerned parents and a confused Maria. Explaining the misunderstanding between them there was laughter all round, though fading quickly as the reality of David's disappearance set in.

The following day saw an improvement in the weather, so much so that once again it also saw the arrival of Detective Chief Inspector Alan Lawson standing on the Martin resident's doorstep, "his rowlocks freezing!" as he so aptly put it.

"Just a formality," he exclaimed eagerly, determined that this time a satisfactory conclusion would adhere, "and one that would offer a reincarnation of his esteem among his fellow officers," he muttered hopefully. "Something that had been lacking for some time!" he acknowledged wistfully.

Wasting little time he asked for permission to search David's room. Which he got! Proceeding with the wardrobe, then the bed and a variation of small draws and cupboards eventually he came to THAT drawer. Amy watched in fascination as the officer meticulously searched each item for clues, her face dropping then turning to horror as the first photo appeared, dropping still further as a picture of a naked

Maria standing brushing her hair in front of her bedroom mirror was presented to her.

"Would I be correct in assuming that your son might posses a little bit more than just brotherly fondness for Maria?" the officer enquired rather cynically, to which the already embarrassed Amy replied with a. "Perhaps he does!"

The third photo caused her to gulp as a shot of Maria and Harry in a naked embrace convinced Amy that David was indeed a pervert, declining the offer to view anymore with a whispered. "No thanks!"

The Inspector seemed delighted with his catch, offering him an insight into the man's mind with the letter acting more as a bonus. "Some very interesting photos we have here Mrs Martin," he coughed, "though the state of the poor man's mind at the time of writing that letter is more worrying," he assured a very concerned and confused Amy, to which Maria nearly choked.

"Poor man!" she remarked in anger, "poor bloody nothing" she growled, her insistence that he was nothing but a perverted freak falling on death ears. The Inspector was not interested in any backstabbing. Little did he know!

Maria stayed in the background, smiling secretively as she remarked, "Well how indigenous the photo in my hand appears to be. This one!" she insisted as she waved the photo for all to see. "The one taken in the garden on a beautiful summer's day," she angered in a submission to make the most from the situation. They looked at her in astonishment, not quite sure what to make of her actions.

"I found it under the bathroom mat only yesterday," she lied. "And not wanting to upset my parents I kept it a secret", she lied again. "But now the truth is out, well! Here it is! That should convince you once and for all that he is a pathetic pervert, with some un-natural and overpowering infatuation for me," she scowled. "I've often caught him looking at me," she exclaimed enthusiastically, "and I'm convinced that more than once it was his face leering at me as I bathed," she grimaced. "Though I couldn't be sure, until now that is! He would offer little chide remarks and intimations about the way I dressed," she sobbed encouragingly, now milking the whole process with an enthused determination that this was her moment of glory and that she would make the most of it. "And more than once his hands had brushed hard against my bottom as I'd lent forwards," she sobbed still more, showing the now more than astonished Inspector the exact spot as lifting her skirt she offered him a glimpse of her lace knickers and Lilly-white right cheek as she drew back the thin fabric for his inspection.

"Look!" she smiled to the enthused detective as Amy put a reassuring hand about her shoulder, "look at the bruising!" The Inspector looked hard! Though there was of course nothing to see as her mother quickly pushed her skirt back in place remarking that, "perhaps the Inspector has seen enough dear." He certainly hadn't!

"Well, there's plenty to go on," remarked the Inspector with a rye smile, his mind focused on the well-rounded bottom he had just had the privilege to inspect. "And I'll initiate a search-party immediately," he assured them, "though after having seen that bottom he had little hesitation in understanding where the search should begin," he smiled to himself enthusiastically. With that the Inspector bid his leave, followed by the two officers whose memory of Maria's nakedness on those photos' would certainly not be forgotten in a hurry. Their eagerness to return was without question!

Amy was in tears, leaving Peter and Sonny to console her while Arthur paced up and down in disbelief. "My own son," he pondered, "how could he do such a thing!" he angered wearily, now more disappointed with his son's perverted actions than showing any concern for his absence. This overly distributed anxiety for David's disappearance had, by mutual consent, taken a realistic backseat in their succession of worries, with their thoughts now directed on the stigma that would be attached when the media attained, "their very own version of the facts" as their father had cynically put it.

"Perhaps if he has committed suicide it might just soften the blow," muttered a disconsolate Amy, having now given up hope of ever seeing her son alive again after reading THAT letter. "Then the public might be a bit more sympathetic to everything that has taken place," she grimaced, as the recollection of the photos sank in.

They lived in hope! Maria didn't give a toss, she knew exactly where he was, "and as for Sonny, she still had to be taught a lesson," she mused angrily, turning her thoughts to Sonny's involvement with Harry and what it had done to her, something that without doubt remained unforgiving and firmly stuck in her mind!

The knock on the door awoke them to the real world as Maria answered, her sigh indicating that it was Roger Richards from next door. "He's come to see if there's any news," she exclaimed to her now perturbed mother, knowing full well that both Roger and his bloody family were just being downright 'fucking nosey'. They had never cared for David in the first place, in fact ever since he'd threatened Roger for daring even so much as to look at Maria. Though gloating might have been more the operative!

There was plenty of news, but not for his ears, he would no doubt find out soon enough. He had also brought over the latest Silurian Lusaka's DVD, the romantic though rather saucy one he had overheard Sonny talking to Maria about only last week, her descriptive recount having more than devoured his appetite to see it for himself!

"Sonny would appreciate it much more than me I'm sure," remarked the unenthused Maria, "and she has a DVD player in her room," she smiled enthusiastically. Maria had a plan to humiliate her, "dear sister!"

Sonny couldn't wait to see the DVD! She had been dieing to see this particular film for ages but couldn't get hold of it, and now she had the opportunity, be it with a boy of eighteen with a spotty face and a little…Well! Maria returned to her room, she had just the thing, the bottle of sacrificial potion she'd found last June, the day after the festival and next to the carcass of that 'chicken incarnate' that had surrendered its soul to the devil. She would give them time to settle and then she would bring up the drinks, with more than a drop of the potion added for good measure.

She waited! "Fifteen minutes should be time enough," she smiled eagerly as she prepared the orange drinks, with a touch of vodka and a good dose of the potion each.

Knocking on Sonny's door she entered, only to find the curtains closed leaving them in darkness and fully engrossed in the film as Sonny lay sprawled across the bed, quite oblivious to the fact that her skirt had risen to well above her backside though the cheeks of her bottom did little to inspire, offering a fleeting approved glance and the occasional grunt from a Roger who remained crouched on the floor to her front in an absorbed conference with Silurian.

"Drinks are on offer," Maria smiled, offering them a jug of her 'special brew' as she followed the film, astounded at the antics displayed remarking, "are you sure it isn't a porno' you're watching?" Sonny laughed as she swallowed the drink in one gulp.

"What the hell is in that?" she questioned the innocent looking Maria, "it's bloody strong!" she smiled in unconcealed satisfaction, "though I certainly need it," she muttered, looking with disgust at Roger picking his nose.

Roger followed suit, his determination not to be beaten apparent as they both asked for a refill. Maria obliged willingly, leaving them the jug as she beat a hasty retreat. "I'll call back later," she exclaimed, "to see if you'd like the jug refilled," she smiled, as closing the door she left them to it.

Sonny's expression changed with each mouthful of the potion, her appetite for sex increasing with both the film and the drink directing her actions. Her skirt had now worked its way up to her shoulders in an enthused response to her emotions, her tight jumper following suit as the effect of the potion took its course. With her emotions running high as her eyes focused on James De Manteca's erect penis feeling its way to between Silurian's heaving loins Sonny's fingers clutched nervously at the elasticised thread supporting knickers that resembled little else than a pink lace thong, though still covering all that was required of them – just for the moment - as the passion of the moment and the need to free herself of this encumbrance to her sexual inclinations encouraged her to remove them forthwith.

Another drink was demanded by a Roger whose increasing desire to experience sex with Sonny had been fuelled both by Sonny's actions and the potion, alongside the erotica being portrayed on the DVD of course. Sonny obliged immediately, laughing innocently as leaning over the bed to fill his glass her breasts rested themselves from her bra to land casually on Roger's head. The rest of her body followed, confronting a delighted Roger to glide gracefully from the bed in a diagnostic insurgence landing naked in a heap across his receptive crutch her bottom expressing all the joys of the moment as twisting sharply she repositioned her posture.

"Good evening!" she laughed her voice slurred and impulsive. "Now fuck me!" she demanded as a further drink was consumed, ripping the clothes from poor Roger's back in a lustful desire to feel the warmth of his - or anyone else's penis for that matter - enter into an unholy communion with the orifice that awaited in a consuming desire to enjoy to its full.

"Fuck me!" she demanded again to the surprised Roger, who thought that at last his moment in time had come and that now he was about to enter the gates to an earthly paradise that had until now eluded him as she grabbed his semi-erect penis in a desperate bid to have sex. It wasn't to be! The limp object was devoid of life as dejectedly she returned to the film, content with amusing herself eventually to collapse on the already prone figure of Roger.

Maria was waiting! "Time!" she muttered to herself excitedly as she crept into the room to discover them both snoring peacefully, out for the count and oblivious to her next move. Laying Sonny to her back she drew back her legs to expose that very same orifice that only a moment before had been so demanding. Then dragging Roger to her side he positioned his face evenly between her groins, placing it firmly within the confines of the thickness of a bush still moist from what might have been. Smiling she readied her camera, angling its position to ensure that a perfect picture would be taken, though oblivious to the shadow in the background. A shadow that would not be noticed until the film's later development!

Leaving them to their sleep she left the room, unaware as to the presence of the strange shadow that loomed over the two unwary figures, its intention leaving no uncertainties having readied itself to exact horrors beyond belief on the prone bodies of poor Sonny and Roger.

The immediate arrival of Detective Chief Inspector Alan Lawson was met with a bout of hysterical screams and whimpering from a distraught Amy.

"I found them both after Maria informed me that she was concerned at the lack of noise from Sonny's bedroom," she exclaimed, sobbing uncontrollably. "With that I remember little, I think I must have fainted," she sobbed again. She had! With dear Peter as usual left to pacify her, having carried her from the horrors confronting him to immediately ring the police.

Concern at the lack of noise had been the last thing on Maria's mind. In fact, Maria had not been concerned in the slightest as after all she had arranged the whole thing in the hope of embarrassing both Sonny and her mother. It had backfired!

Sonny had survived unscathed though was still in a state of shock, as for Roger! Peter showed them to the bedroom; a bedroom where the Devil himself could easily have sought refuge and where the sight of Roger's naked body lay in a disfigured contortion against the wall, his head battered beyond all recognition his eyes hanging from sockets that offered themselves to their mortality. The flesh had been ripped and torn from his blooded torso as the savagery of the attack struck home.

"What in hell's name took place here," remarked the increasingly pale Inspector, his inability to comprehend expressed clearly on a face now ashen and drawn. "This carnage is something that only some epitome of the devil could possibly have achieved," he stuttered, scratching his head nervously. "It's as if something from hell was attempting to drag the very soul from his body," continued the horrified Inspector Lawson, his face contorted in revulsion his body convulsed as running to the bathroom he was violently sick.

"Another case to solve," the mortified Inspector acknowledged as he glanced at the short trail of earth and mud leading from the window, his face strained and haggard, recognising his fallibility as he realised that here was another gruesome state of affairs that could yet again prove to be another unsolvable case.

"Three deaths at the Martin residence with one suspected suicide and the death of a workman at the mill, what the hell is going on?" he mused in a disconcerted effort to understand the situation. "No human being could possibly have inflicted such horrendous injuries in such a short space of time, and certainly no human could have entered and departed unseen, unheard, no footprints, and without any physical or material evidence to offer even the slightest of clues to their being. Just that damn trail of clay and mud," he muttered in despair.

"I can't recall anything," whispered the inconsolable Sonny to the Inspector. "Just the sight of poor Roger lying there," she stammered, trying to gather her senses. "I came over funny after drinking that bloody orange," she explained. "Maria!" she muttered.

"The orange will be taken away for analysis, along with further samples of the clay and earth," remarked the Inspector, assuring Amy that everything possible would be done to solve all of the crimes that had taken place in the household, and not just this one. "And as for you young lady, what the hell did you put in their drink?" he remarked, looking at Maria angrily.

She was left with little choice but to explain in full her intentions, presenting the remnants of the potion for its analysis, to which the Inspector found himself offered with little alternative but to caution her immediately, although remaining convinced that there was no obvious reason for this very attractive though stupid girl to be involved in any such murder.

"All the same, investigations and an enquiry would be called for to ratify his expressed opinion," he emphasised quietly, looking at Maria for any sign of a reaction. There was none! Though the arrival of an ambulance churning up the frozen snow as it skidded to a halt outside the mill-cottage brought home to them all the reality of the situation and how treacherous conditions outside still were.

Normal procedures were followed, with the usual tedious routine involving all investigative measures leaving all those involved with, as expected. Nothing! Nothing new at least!

The whole bizarre situation was taking its toll on the Inspector as back at his office once again he attempted to come up with some sort of explanation "No new leads to follow, no conclusions to be drawn, just an explanation of the obvious! The three murders at the mill-cottage had all involved sex. The two family members directly involved had been spared the experience of some horrifying death. And of course, that bloody clay trail," he sighed, his spirit to continue in further investigations of any sort falling by the second.

"Some unearthly presence appears to have endorsed a directive that each female inhabitant who had, at sometime in their lives, involved themselves in some form of satanic ritual, and in doing so had perhaps inadvertently offered their souls to the Devil," the Inspector deduced thoughtfully, [offering reference to the initiations]. "And are being conserved for something far greater, though for what!" he groaned again, glancing at his clock wearily. "A feature that would include both Sonny, Maria, and their mother!" he concluded pragmatically, having deduced little if anything in such reasoning.

"This all seems preposterous, ludicrous in fact," he sighed, as scratching his head he reflected once again on the accounts of each murder. "Perhaps when they find David - or his body - fresh light will be thrown on the situation", he reflected, though with little enthusiasm to such a conjecture.

It was then that something clicked. "Of course, it was the year nineteen hundred and ninety nine, and next year would be the year of the millennium. Would the fact that it would be the first solstice of a new millennium offer any indication as to why the womenfolk at the mill-cottage had had their lives spared! What did that mysterious earthy- clay trail indicate! That sacrificial potion that Maria had used! Why! Did Maria hold the key to the whole sordid business?" He wondered!

And so the baffled Inspector continued to ponder on these speculations well into the night as the annoying chimes from THAT clock - a clock that he had been stupid enough to recently purchase - indicated that it was 5am. "And what about that folk-tail, the one of the death of a young girl during building operations all those years ago!" he asked himself. "A death that had encouraged her un-avenged spirit to seek its revenge on those associated with the mill! Was there any truth in it?" He rubbished such ideas with an annoyed grunt, with his thoughts completely lost in the complicated web that had widened as he dictated his concerns, presumptions and ideas to tape.

"Then there was always that 'Druid's Stone'," he gasped, "that legend that went with it of the stone's ability to yield some sort of un-natural strength and virility! And. The sacrificial offering and initiation to the 'Sun God'!" he speculated. "All Hocus-pocus," he mused despondently, "who would believe such rubbish and what about my street credibility?" he growled angrily, his thoughts directed at the reverence that had been bestowed upon him by his fellow officers. "That would unquestionably take a tumble if my views were ever made public." And still he continued to ponder, unsure as to his reasoning behind anything, but still, "he was bloody well determined not to be beaten. He would have to do his own detective work, in secret and when the time was ripe!"

Chapter VI

And so again life went on at Millrise cottage, though normality seemed a mile away, with not only the family but the neighbours and the locals finding it difficult to come to terms with what had taken place, leaving the villagers now considering the cottage not only as haunted but, as 'A House of Evil'. The local vicar had offered to intervene, even as far as offering to exorcise the cottage and mill; something that had been flatly turned down by an angry Arthur, whose Pagan beliefs did little in entertaining all such 'man made religions' as he considered those such as Christianity and Islam to be.

"Mother Nature and the universal elements that drive it are all that we should be looking at," he had always considered, "with the sun and the moon dictating all we need to know," he would smile secretly, his face twisting unnaturally as if communicating with some infinitive entity who held countenance over all Earth's ills.

"Perhaps he was right!" Maria had always considered, her feelings on his beliefs often holding foundation, with a Maria who looked upon all religions as nothing but troublesome and meddling relics of man's need to dominate.

Suspicion and accusing fingers did little to help, though a concerted public relations exercise orchestrated by Arthur had helped in easing the tension that had existed within the community, with the village elders seemingly intent in seeing that the Martin family should in no way be hounded, but instead should be given reassurance and words of encouragement and comfort. As to why, the family hadn't a clue, though Maria's instinct had been to accept that it must be necessary.

David's body had finally been discovered, with obvious conclusions having been drawn. "He had committed suicide by throwing himself down the mineshaft, impaling himself on a jagged rock as he fell or on landing," beamed the Inspector to his assistant, having ascertained the situation admirably, though with little thought given to the Martin family's feelings. The Inspector could at last congratulate himself on something.

"Case solved!" Maria had smiled wryly on hearing the verdict. "How could they all be so bloody stupid," she wondered, her eye transfixed on the Inspector as the judge congratulated him on his investigative prowess, his face wary and fatigued though a rye smile enough to indicate a touch of relief on at least one judgment he could satisfy himself with.

"A fucking monkey could have done just as well," she scowled, having taken an instant dislike to this arrogant and presumptuous detective, who at thirty-two remained the youngest Detective Chief Inspector ever experienced within the county. "Although he is very good looking," she smiled encouragingly, responding immediately by questioning herself for such tenuous thoughts.

Peter was due to get married in May and, Maria was jealous! Her fondness for her dear stepbrother had developed into something more physical, more fortuitous than even she could have accepted; having decided that such feelings would be considered morally improper, though deep down remaining fearful that perhaps a point had been reached where these very same feelings could now be considered as way beyond her control. Now it was something more consuming, more passionate though Peter would never know, at least not just yet!

Sonny was engaged, engaged to a big hulking builder who was as thick as the proverbial but had a heart of gold. She loved him! Her mother and father appeared happy enough, but as for herself! She was absolutely fed up. She would be twenty in three months time, and although she could have almost any man she desired she had still not found her 'Mr Right'. Both she and Sonny were now on speaking terms, having balanced out their differences with Maria's spiking of her drink and the ensuing murder condensing Sonny's flirtation with poor Harry.

"Not a very favourable balance," Sonny had smiled at her defensive sister, "but certainly a welcome one," she laughed as she gave Maria a big hug. They were friends again!

A small number of early migrating birds had returned to a welcoming warm spell that had cleared the snow and ice in a frenzied attack by the 'Sun God'. First blooms of a spring that not long ago had seemed a very unlikely prospect now poked inquisitively from the moist clay-soil in the hope that no late frost would catch them off guard, and, offering new hope to the many insects that had remained underground to live out their lives secure from the frozen earth above.

Maria welcomed this sight with an enthusiastic yawn as she considered her options. "To tender her resignation as a nanny and enter the academic world of Bristol University or, to move away completely and try to make a new life for herself!" she mused silently, feeling unable to decide on either as for a moment her eyes closed, dazzled by the brightness of a sun that seemed to enjoy playing games, its penetrating rays playing casually across her face. The 'Sun God' had looked down at her as if deciding that her options were without foundation. She had none! Her life - at least for the near future - would remain within the village. She would secure a job at the village stores and any notion of an academic future - or any other for that matter - would be put on hold. 'The Sun God' had spoken! Turning away from the sun's rays she closed her eyes. "Had she been dreaming?"

Chapter VII

The year two thousand had arrived bringing mixed fortunes for the Martin family, but even so, the new millennium had caused great excitement in the village. For a small number of villagers however irrational thinking had superseded logic, with their excitement blending within an aurora of proportions as the occasion of the first solstice of the twenty-first century offered more than just the opportunity of a fine display of fireworks on the village green. More even than a barbecue, a bonfire and a various number of displays by local groups encouraged by a visiting troupe of Morris dancers that lent their own individual enchantment to what a quaint Devonshire village was all about. They had other more sinister things on their minds! However, to most the main attraction would be the featuring of a visiting 'fun-fare'.

The Druid Stone' had remained isolated throughout the winter, its calm serenity offering a benign indifference though eagerly awaiting its big chance to stand proud once again. But this year, this year it would be putting on a show of exceptional proportions, a show that would prove once and for all that its Pagan foundations outshone all of mankind's modern theological thinking.

Preparations for the festival had already commenced, with rehearsals for the parade through the village having already taken place and coinciding with the acquisition of the visiting fare. The purchase of the fireworks had been budgeted in accordance with their importance alongside the ordering of a bountiful supply of food and drink, and of course, the detailed adeptness that went in the layout of the bonfire with the sacrificial homage's importance being held within a communion of secrecy that those chosen to pay homage to the 'Stone' and the 'Sun God' would recognize definitely.

The grand finale would of course be the initiation ceremony, with its once innocent intention now lying in tatters after last year's incongruous charade that had been the main topic of conversation within the community for the weeks following. Even so, the advent of the new millennium would not be complete without something of particular significance taking place, and behind the scenes arrangements were indeed taking place for such a domiciliary event.

Maria worked hard at the village stores. It was certainly not a job she would normally have chosen but her instincts led her to believe that at least until after the summer period this was the job for her. Regularly she would visit the stone, to wonder at its origin and how it came about, her fascination and keenness to delve into its mysteries growing by the week. This unnatural fascination became almost ritualistic, with an increasing interest being shown in an assortment of ancient rituals stemming from devil worship, black and white magic to various foreign cults and beliefs that she had almost unconsciously taken to reading about.

Her family remained puzzled and concerned at Maria's newly found obsession with such dangerous activities, having experienced for themselves either directly or indirectly such practices, and were well aware of how things could easily get out of hand. Maria, they thought would be the last person to involve herself in such questionable divergences, but how wrong could they be! Some driving force seemed keen to embrace her spirit, to encompass her within a protective shield and to supersede her natural instincts and inquisitiveness! At times she was not her own person, didn't belong, was vague and unresponsive and certainly not the Maria that they all knew and loved.

Detective Chief Inspector Alan Lawson was not beyond doing his very own 'personalised' detective work, and especially when his job was on the line and his credibility as 'an officer who could show results' was concerned. The mill seemed a good place to start, with perhaps samples of the soil taken at levels slightly deeper than previously achieved offering him somewhat more than just 'a ray of hope'.

He remained convinced that those trails left at each of the murder scenes originated from somewhere around the mill's foundations, and, that with the aid of a good spade he could attempt to retrieve samples of the earth a good three feet down and a good twelve inches further than originally had been prescribed. From there he would scrutinise every last bit of detailed information available on the 'Druid Stone', with implicit analysis of its surrounds and rock substance. If that didn't help he was prepared to put his life at risk as bait to attract the killer's primal instincts, to offer himself as the intended victim to whatever it was committing these murders. Although not without the knowledge that a number of handpicked officers would offer a screen of almost watertight security, lying in wait and ready to pounce at a moments notice.

"Somehow he must entice Maria into unwittingly colluding with his plan, initiate some means whereby he could seduce her into wanting him and offering herself as a sexual partner," he concluded hopelessly, without any real thought being given into what he, a police officer and upholder of the law could possibly offer such a beautiful creature, his thinking denying him any form of rational reasoning.

But he was desperate! "And it must be in her bedroom!" he insisted to himself without any logical conclusion. He hadn't failed to notice how Maria had been looking at him on the occasions of his visits, and, he was sure that he could 'win her over' if he tried hard enough.

⊰⊱

"If all failed it was back to the drawing board and most probably the loss of his job!" he muttered, having withdrawn into the world of fiction's top sleuths, with his beloved 'Sherlock Holmes' offering him some glimmer of hope and directive.

Maria had undoubtedly found herself attracted to this good-looking man, though his arrogant and self-opinionated attitude had annoyed her. But somehow, somehow that quaint sort of acquiescent charm of his, alongside a tall, well-built frame enhancing rugged features that boasted a cleft chin and dark brown eyes - a package that in all could well simulate what might be considered as a well rehearsed attachment to the typical James Bond figure - had her considering him more than a challenge than anything else. And, she remained open to any suggestions that he could well put forward to her of anything that could possibly resemble 'a date'.

"After all, he must have his weaknesses," she grinned in acceptance that she was sure of her own conclusions, "and all men are fallible in the face of a beautiful women's charms," she accepted, knowing only too well that she had the attributes worthy of such a statement.

"And let's face it," she pondered passionately, "he might be a Detective Chief Inspector but so what. He wasn't married! Didn't appear to have a steady! And by all accounts was certainly good in bed. So what had she got to lose!" she muttered assertively, denouncing any thoughts she may have had to the contrary with a rueful smile.

"Certainly not her virginity," she continued dispassionately, "that went years ago at just seven years of age. Her dignity! That had floundered since the occasion of that bloody initiation. Though she still retained her self-pride. But! He certainly had more to offer than most of the men she'd encountered. No! If Alan Lawson made a move in her direction she would most certainly reciprocate," her objective desires seemingly oozing enthusiasm.

From the shadows of a full moon a strange and un-decisive figure crept incongruously from behind a clump of bushes, heading hesitantly in the direction of a grassed bank that sank steeply towards the fast flowing stream at its base. The Inspector, with spade in hand, proceeded to dig at the mill's foundations in a desperate bid to extract any further evidence that might come to hand; evidence that might offer a connection between the mill and that trail left in the two bedrooms at the mill-cottage - though still remaining completely unaware that such a trail had also been left in the kitchen at the time of the removal of David's body, and, at the mouth of the mineshaft - . But still! Did it matter?

By the light of the moon he spent the best part of an hour in his frenzied attempt to finally convince the world that the murderer had made its home there, and that deep down in the clay deposit evidence of that very fact would soon come to light. He remained exhausted, and having dug a good four feet into the bank he was satisfied that the substance he'd extracted bore a strong resemblance to those very same earth and clay sediments left in the trail. Now his finding would be taken for his own personal analysis, and, satisfaction.

"Satisfaction at last" he muttered excitedly to the moon, deciding that the simplistic smile that beamed down at him must be nothing less than a look of approval.

Next he approached the field where there the 'Druid Stone' stood glaring in a tone of disapproval and obstinacy from its solitary position in a dense area of thicket and shrub that had paid homage to its well being for all those centuries. Its sibyl understanding with long lost spirits denouncing a mere mortal's intrusion on its importance as the Inspector proceeded to extract scrapings of the rock from its cragged surface. For a moment the Inspector stopped, he could feel the wind reaching out to him, searching his soul in whispered gusts as if echoing some deep dark message from the stone.

"I dare you to continue!" was its simple message, "and if you do…well!" The Inspector shivered!

The Stone remained pacified in a refrained diversion to this infliction to its dignity as the wind increased, to lash the surrounding trees and flora as if commanding that attention should be paid to its powers and to welcome the ethereal figure of a little girl as she approached from the mill's direction. She showed little concern as the Inspector retreated deep into the shadows, his gaze focused in suspended animated horror on the characterise translucency of what could only be conceived as a ghost as it sought to dance in a pragmatic defiance to gravity about the stone.

"I must be dreaming," agonised the poor Inspector as he pinched himself. He wasn't! The shrouded figure appeared to glide effortlessly towards the stone as if drawn by some unseen force to its surface, melting within the confounds of its being leaving a dazzling magnetic aurora to emit its magnificence in an optical illusion of colour as its secret drew on its desire to protect the asylum of the child. The Inspector drew back both in amazement and horror, his disbelief offering itself to the incredulity of the situation as rubbing his eyes he lost himself to the wonderment of the situation.

"Had he actually witnessed these events," he pondered, his thoughts circulating in an ever-decreasing circle with the one word, "impossible," offered as a subtle reasoning behind it all. "He was not focusing right! His mind was confused and disorientated with the strain of the murder cases inflicting this torture to his soul. "He would go for the last option," he almost shouted as he ran from the scene. "That should prove them all wrong," he laughed in a hysterical burst to his own defence. "He would offer the proof necessary to condemn those who spoke outright that some 'out of this world entity' had transcended from its satanic temple way beneath the earth's crust, and would prove once and for all that this sadistic and brutal killer was indeed. Human!"

Chapter VIII

Peter Martin was about to get married, and family and friends had gathered at the tiny village church of St Mary's to welcome the arrival of the couple as they prepared to join in holy matrimony with the possibility of one day owning a five hundred acre farm. Love was certainly on the agenda, but future prospects left Peter in no doubt that this was the girl for him. Maria looked on in an admiring jealousy to the bride, determined that one day a loving father would be escorting HER down the isle and on to her adoring bridegroom, though with all her heart wishing it could have been her beloved Peter. She could dream! The service was short but sweet with her mother consistently crying throughout, leaving Maria to show her annoyance at such an emotional stance that rightfully belonged to her.

"After all, it was she that was suffering not the bloody bride," she groaned helplessly.

"Sonny would be next," she announced dejectedly to the industrious little spider that had satisfied itself that an empty pew served admirably to catch its unwary prey. "But as for her? What hope did she have, every bloody boyfriend that had come her way had either died or no doubt would have died if she'd brought him home," she reminded the spider, who saw fit to ignore her remarks having decided that a tasty fly proved the more acceptable of the two options. "But the Inspector, now here was an opportunity not to be missed. Who in their right mind would kill a Detective Chief Inspector!" she mused, glancing towards the unsuspecting detective sitting quietly in the pews as she smiled that same adhering smile that had won over all the boys, and, the Inspector would not be without his failings.

"She would see him back at the cottage," she whispered in acknowledgment to his nod, as again she whispered that, "he could be on hand if another murder occurred." He smiled! Little did she know!

Up until now May had been a beautiful month, and, up until now the 12th May had been a beautiful day. The 'Sun God' had been smiling down at them and the spirits had seen fit to endorse the marriage with a feeling of well being, and, a gratuity that would offer dividends to their future happiness. The wedding reception was held in the cottage grounds, and a large marquee had been erected for the occasion with a live band, plenty of food and drink and a host of light entertainment including a magician to keep both the children and a number of the adults suspended to their seats as a fine display of magical wizardry was performed. Though the disappearance of the magician left more than wonderment not only to the children but the adults as well! His intoxicated state had finally got the better of him, leaving him collapsed behind the props in a drunken heap oblivious to all around.

Peter and his bride had arrived in a horse and carriage, and one that had been especially decorated for the occasion looking resplendent in a multitude of streamers, balloons, and a varying number of bells and other oddments that enhanced the whole atmosphere with an overriding exuberance befitting the happy event. The joyful couple had adhered to their promise that Maria would be guaranteed 'that' bouquet the bride had dispatched with enthusiasm to the enthralled young girls awaiting their opportunity for their turn to address the alter in holy matrimony, and sure enough, she hadn't been disappointed!

"Though now that Peter was married it had all been just a meaningless gesture," she'd sighed, with her thoughts turning to what could have been her body tingling at such futile expectations.

The late afternoon extended into an early evening that saw fireworks and the early departures of those guests that had some distance to travel. Alcohol was consumed in quantity, with Alan Lawson insisting that Maria should get the full benefits of a fine Devonshire cider that certainly had some 'poke' to it. The evening continued with a swing, with the Inspector having made great inroads in his quest to seduce Maria into an inspection of her bedroom, "to ensure that all was safe," he coughed unconvincingly.

"She felt safe and fully at ease with this charming and witty man," she sighed to a surprised Sonny, who had been baffled at Maria's insistence that the Inspector could offer her something that a number of the other equally charming and good looking men at the party couldn't.

"It was the fact that he was a Detective Chief Inspector," she announced to a startled Sonny, now fully convinced that her adopted sister was either mad or too drunk to know her own mind. She was certainly tipsy, but her desire to be held and loved once again and to have complete peace of mind if he did insist that her room would offer a secure place for…! "Well, why not!" Her desire to be loved once again, and, seemingly by a gentleman, overshadowed any concerns she may have had that once again the killer might strike. "Who in their right mind would even consider the murder of a Detective Chief Inspector, even if he happened to be off duty!" she mused confidently.

Off duty! Little did she know!! Tonight she could at last free herself from her inhibitions; free from the shackles impeding her sexual requirements, feeling secure in the knowledge that if any harm came to this man then the full wrath of the Devonshire constabulary would descend to vent its anger on the perpetrator. "If only he would ask her!"

His mind was made up. The whole scenario lent itself to the possibility that tonight the killer might strike once again. Maria would unknowingly be the bait, as would he, and any reservations he may have had that he was 'using her' far outweighed the importance he put on his future in the force and, his self-esteem.

"Whoever or whatever it was that had been doing these killings was certain not to miss this opportunity," he decided wholeheartedly, and he was prepared to make quite obvious his intentions though using a slightly more subtle approach. Just enough to attract the attention of the killer, if indeed he made an appearance! Or, if he'd got wind that tonight conditions would be perfect for the type of perverse reasoning he had for committing such heinous acts of self-gratification.

The scene had been set, with a number of plain-clothes officers mingling with the unsuspecting guests and several more outside of the cottage keeping watch. For what they weren't sure, just anything that looked suspicious was the agreed consensus. Drink followed drink as Mara's jealousy of her brother continued.

"Of course she was happy for both of them, but her beloved Peter, gone for good!" she sighed. "It was too much to bear," she hastened as her moist eyes filled to offer an occasional teardrop that made its way leisurely down her cheek.

"And, to leave her, his adoring Maria to her misery whilst he chose to live in the recently refurnished and refurbished farm cottage with his new bride!" she continued as further tears ensued!

"And, the very same one paid for by the bride's parents who had insisted to Peter that nothing was too good for their dear daughter, or of course for himself!" she sobbed persistently, the tears increasing leaving a concerned Inspector Lawson to offer his arm in a comforting gesture of goodwill.

Her head rested against his chest as tearfully she informed him of her fondness for her brother, though refraining to tell him how she really felt.

"Please, please don't cry my dear," he motioned consolingly, his old English charm demanding that every effort to comfort this desirable young lady should not be wasted, though trying to understand her predicament was proving more than difficult even for a man who prided himself on first understanding a beautiful girl before ascribing to any enveloping desires.

"Peter's her brother," were his thoughts, "though her adopted brother," he accepted thoughtfully, as smiling he ran his fingers through the fine locks of auburn hair that hung suggestively across Maria's bare shoulders in a submissive acknowledgement to his touch, his lips reaching to hers in a demonstrative expression of his understanding as their eyes met.

"She was his for the taking," he acknowledged as the fullness of lips moist with a passion and longing to engage in heavenly combat with his found their intended target as they embraced.

"She was his to do as he wished," he smiled, as they made their way to her room in a consuming passion of the moment, elated that his charm had succeeded in subscribing to his plan. Though not failing to recognise what dangers might lay before them. "Such beauty!" he sighed as he glanced wistfully towards Maria's smiling face.

"She was his to do as he wished," he acknowledged as undressing her to immortalise the beauty that lay before him he found the softness of breasts demanding to be caressed.

"And, she was his to do as he…!" he stuttered in disbelief, his eyes diverted at the horror emanating before him; the horror that reigned down blows to his head in an indiscriminate frenzy of hate and loathing. No longer was she his to do as he wished as his body lurched towards her in a spasmodic expression of its demise, his head twisted and torn in a disfigured contortion as the sinews of a neck inverted sprung like coiled springs to catch the blood as it oozed unremitting from the smashed remnants of his skull.

He would never know what killed him, but Maria had seen the unearthly spectre of the child as it swirled inconsolably about his person, tearing and scratching at the obtrusive form that had commanded it to his soul as its hands compressed the skull in a display of strength unequalled by earthly mortals. Within an instance the ethereal figure had disbursed into the shadows unobserved as the window closed tight, leaving poor Maria to look on more in astonishment than anything else, fascinated at this creature's exactness and persistence to ensure that nothing was left to chance.

"Detective Chief Inspector Alan Lawson was certainly dead," she muttered, now in a traumatized disbelief at what had just taken place, though her stunned acceptance that she had been party to such a horrific event forced her to stutter, "and nobody would know who had killed him and how, apart from me!" Something that again she announced only this time more decisively, as if proud of being in such a privileged position as her confused brain fought to reinstate its sanity!

Once again her eyes focused on the body in an unremitting desire to scream, her voice restricted by the awfulness of the situation as she ran from the room in a disjointed discord of her belief as to what she had just experienced.

Standing to the top of the stairs Maria's mind again dwelt back to the terror she had just perceived as in an uncontrolled display of both fear and remorse her hysterical screams echoed into the night; a night that had embraced the killer in a consumed acknowledgement to its intent, leaving the solitary owl hooting its condolences to the victim as its eyes focused on the unfortunate field mouse that soon was to be its next intended victim.

Police rushed from all directions, but they were too late. Unannounced restrictions had animated their mortal form, delaying their access to the scene thus allowing Maria the means of escape.

Their unfortunate Chief Inspector would not be announcing his satisfaction at having caught the murderer red handed.

He would not be congratulating himself on "a job well done."

He would not be seeking to re-establish his position within the force.

No! His soulless eyes would be staring at them from a skull that had compressed to the inner sanctum of its being, to expose the grey matter that had devised its own end. He would be telling them. Nothing!

"Who in hell would believe her; believe what they would undoubtedly consider as the ravings of some hysterical girl lost within her own wild imagination if she gave them a detailed account of what had happened and what she had seen. And in graphic detail too! No! They were bound to believe that finally she had lost what little sanity remained if the word ghost was so much as hinted at. Even so, their understanding that she could have devised such an undertaking on her own would surely be deemed as ludicrous. But with an accomplice who just happened to be the killer? well!" she was not so sure.

"After all, who's to say that they might consider her as to be that naïve that she let herself be coerced into assisting in such an undertaking, and if so, well, that could prove a different matter altogether!" she considered thoughtfully. "They were surely not that stupid as to take on board her insistence that the ghastly mutilation of the Inspector could have been done without her seeing? Of course they weren't," muttered Maria almost incoherently, beginning to question her own belief that indeed she was not the killer, though certainly having little intention in letting them think that she was!

"Perhaps she was mad! Or perhaps she was living in some nightmarish state and would eventually awaken to find that it had been just that," were her thoughts as they continued to question her, convinced that she was lying and, that she had been lying in the past. Question after question was put to her with her response being just the same.

"She was innocent! She was not in that room! She was not behind the killings! She did not have an accomplice! And! She could see no reasoning or motive for the murders! Yes! Each of the victims in some way had been associated with her, but so what! Both her mother and Sonny had also been involved in some way and, they had both been in the vicinity as had her father. But, but it didn't prove their guilt!" she continued tearfully.

A squad car had been called for, and with little choice a grief stricken Maria was hastily transferred to the local Constabulary where there she was met by the family solicitor called for by her overly concerned father. But further interrogation proved futile, and with no finger to point to the fact that she was actually in the room at the time of the murder, police bail was agreed.

A suspect she may have been, but her being on the landing - be it scantily dressed - proved little in establishing that she was the murderer or even an accomplice to such an assumption. Indeed, any trace that would indicate that she may even have been in her room at the time of such a gruesome crime could not be established. Her clothes had been found neatly stacked in the bathroom, unblemished though slightly moist from a still steamed up shower cubicle and, with a steady drip of warm water emitting from the shower every indication that Maria had just showered proved an accepted fact. And with no evidence on Maria to indicate a struggle or anything close to such, they had been left with little choice but to caution her, with strict instructions not to leave the village but to ensure that she remained available for any additional questioning that might be required. Her guardian Angel had indeed been watching over her!

The strain was beginning to tell as again she burst into tears, now convinced that she had been used in some way by the Inspector to try and catch the killer, "or why would there be so many plains-clothes police on hand at the time," she insisted to the Assistant Chief Inspector between sobs as she awaited the arrival of her father to take her home. Assistant Chief Inspector Conrad declined to offer any information that might discredit still further his dead partner, though quick to hasten that they'd received a tip off that the killer could strike that night. Maria had her doubts!

"And that still didn't excuse the Chief Inspector for putting her in such mortal danger," she muttered angrily to herself, now showing little sympathy for the dead officer who she considered as having gone way beyond the call of duty, though now careful not to show any indication that she may have been willing to participate in any sexual orientation with the Inspector. "After all, how could they prove it, she was being protected!" she smirked inwardly to herself in satisfaction, now fully convinced that this was indeed the case.

"A tip off that some ghostly creature would attempt to kill and mutilate the Inspector and perhaps her, and, with no apparent motive! Who was he kidding!" she muttered angrily.

Back at the cottage she remained in her room, to be comforted by Sonny whose own experiences led her to believe that for some unknown reason something or someone - although ensuring that THEY remained unharmed - was intent in seeing that any relationship that they pursued within the cottage would be dealt with swiftly. And, in reminding Maria that

neither was their mother exempt, with her recollection of Tom's death poor Maria was reduced to tears, acknowledging such a hurtful reminder with, "and don't I bloody well know!"

"Though what in hell was the connection," Sonny continued! "It was as if each of them was being preserved for something very special, very special indeed!" she queried with her sister, leaving Maria to nod in agreement.

Chapter IX

With just one week to go before the advent of the millennium summer solstice excitement was growing in the village and surrounding area. Doubts about the continuation of such a festival had been dismissed out of hand. The revenue for the village was far too great to warrant any abandonment of such an important occasion, and, with the fiasco of the previous year every effort would go into improving its image though the spirit of the event must remain "Sacra cant".

"After all, no one had ever been hurt during the initiations - at least not physically - and the decision to hold 'the renewal of vows' and an undertaking of allegiance to the 'Sun God' - be it in a light hearted way or otherwise - would be held in the early hours of the morning," agreed the organisers and the village elders between them. "We could ensure that only those who were committed followers of the cult and ones who took it seriously should be in attendance, with the preparation of an enormous fire and more than one altar erected to ensure that the increased volume of new participants could be safely handled," they finally concluded.

The local constabulary had been coerced - though be it with little more than congenial persuasion affording the necessary mandate - into turning a blind eye to the whole occurrence, based on a commitment given by the organisers that only those that had a genuine concept of the whole procedure, and that were made aware of the possible dangers and prepared to accept the consequences should mistakes be made, would be allowed to participate. And finally, that a declaration exonerating the police to that effect should be drawn up and approved by the now newly endorsed Detective Chief Inspector Conrad. Though as to whether any such undertaking contained any viable legal sustenance was another matter! It still remained down to the Inspector.

"Well! There'll be no problems on that score," piped up an enthused organiser. "Inspector Conrad was himself initiated a number of years ago, and remains a keen advocate of all village traditions," he continued, his voice extending into a high pitched squeak in a congratulatory acceptance of the information he'd acquired. His assumptions had proved to be correct! The Detective Chief Inspector had indeed been initiated, having risen through the ranks from constable to his present position with a keenness to ensure that such pagan dialogue would continue unabated. He signed his approval willingly!

The early summer had remained warm and sunny, with the animal and plant life having once again established a firm hold on the surrounding countryside. From her bedroom window once again Maria scanned the horizon, re-establishing memories of happier times when Tom had struggled his way along the garden path in that storm, and Peter had rescued her from her imagination on the night she'd remained convinced that a rapist had been following her.

"Oh how she missed her beloved Peter!" she mused disconcertedly. "With his happy, cheerful face about the house, his witty jokes and concerns, but above all his sense of loyalty to the family!" she smiled comfortably. "No matter what he would always be there to comfort or console, to stick by his parents in their hour of need, even at the time of their mother making a complete idiot of herself," she scoffed in un-amused distain as she reflected on the moment. Something that still played on her mind and continued to annoy her!

"He idolised Sonny of course, as after all she was his 'real sister' were in contrast she remained unrelated, except by proxy. As for his feelings towards her, well! She wasn't sure! She knew that Peter's love for his wife wasn't real. He had told her so - though not in so many words - but enough to convince her after that occasion he'd found her crying in her bedroom.

It had been soon after he'd announced to the family that he was going to be married. Maria had always looked upon their relationship as something special, and, as his non biological sister had always considered that perhaps there might be something more than just good, solid friendship. In a moment of weakness putting such theories to the test had left her floundering with embarrassment, having let her feelings towards him slip from lips tightening as each stuttered word was uttered within a haze of uncontrollable passion as she sought any answer that might give her hope. But unfortunately for a poor Maria hope was not forthcoming! He had declined to answer, just offering her a smile and a wink as closing the door softly behind him he had left her to her feelings.

She had seen herself in that very same carriage occupied by the newly married couple, only with herself as the bride. Her jealous mind envisaging the two horses as they drew this 'chariot of lovers' from the church to the cottage, it's leisurely pace capturing the freshness of a narrow country lane that exuded charm and vitality, swallowing the fragrances that the local flora offered to the eager recipients as holding Her hand Peter had told his bride, his bride Maria - not that Fiona whose wealthy parents doted on and who would without question ensure that their financial future would remain secure - how much he loved her.

"He was lying! He loved her! He loved her and one day THEY must get married," she sobbed, though deep down knowing that it would never be.

The arrival of the 'fun fare' brought great excitement, especially to the children whose memories of the occasion would live on. The village had never experienced such frivolity as the endless stream of amusements and experiences trooped towards a field that had been set aside for the entertainment. The Carousel as usual was the youngster's favourite, offering rides on hobby horses, racing cars, and bat-mobiles in an ever consuming desire to present a more modern approach to this generation old 'Magic Roundabout'. Maria watched the proceedings with excitement and some degree of sadness. She had never had the opportunity to experience these delights having spent most of her childhood in misery. But! She was determined to make up for her loss as she followed the spinning wheel and big dipper being assembled in a mini offering of what Blackpool could offer, though perhaps not on such grandeur scale!

The young men waved to her and she waved back enthusiastically, whilst their women-folk scowled and offered postulating and indicative responses of their own. Maria posed a threat and didn't they know it. Not one of them could match her beauty or figure, and even though several of the girls could easily flirt with a Latin come Gypsy appearance that would knock any man off his feet, they could not compete with the charm and elegance that Maria had to offer. Their scowls increased as she allowed herself time to gaze adoringly at their strapping young men-folk stripped to the waist, their bronzed muscles glistening in a sheen of sweat as the 'Sun God' offered its blessing to their arrival. They would not be disappointed!

Two days to the millennium solstice and the heat and excitement was building to a crescendo. Three large white altars had been erected between the fire and the 'Druid Stone', depicting in its way the crucifixion and proclamation of Christ's existence though comparing little in its intention. Alongside each a short, narrow wooden-stake had been driven into the earth, around which a mound of sticks and heather had been built offering the semblance of sacrificial fires ready and awaiting the introduction of their dead chickens!

The 'Druid Stone' had been patiently biding its time in anticipation of its big moment, to enter into a spiritual bonding once again with its mentor, to stimulate the souls of those long lost spirits that had offered themselves to the guru of all heavenly clusters as it watched over mother earth with a heartfelt affiliation to the life it supported. Those very same spirits would now have the opportunity to relinquish their shackles, to return to their earthly institute once again and repay their gratitude for their mortality to the 'Sun God'. They would enter into a holy sacrament as they offered atonement for their misdemeanours, exacting extolment from THEIR God in a show of gratitude for their being. But! There was something else!

"My head!" muttered Sonny as she entered the kitchen where Maria was busy washing up. "What a horror of a dream that was," she announced to the Royal Dalton china cup that had fallen from Maria's grasp to land in pieces on the floor.

"Fuck!" cursed an annoyed Maria, whose recount of her own dream left Sonny astonished. Though the word dream might be considered unworthy of such horrors swirling deep within the minds of two girls who had both experienced nothing less than the mother of all nightmares; nightmares running parallel not only to each other but to that of Amy's, whose pale face as she peered round the kitchen door said it all. "She was shit scared!"

Fear turned to fascination as they compared their dreams later that day, with each finding that the basis of their nightmare bore strong similarities, though with their essence differing slightly in its contradiction.

"It's only a bloody dream," laughed Sonny nervously, having agonised over its contents for a moment, "though certainly scary enough," she acknowledged, her mind pondering on its possible significance but still unable to draw any conclusion.

And so talk of the dream continued within the clarity of subdued whispers. Maria was still twenty, and as the youngest her youth would be savoured by those who wished to inflict harm. Sonny would have the same courtesy extended to her, though her suffering would be more intense. But as for their poor mother! She would receive the wrath of Satan himself as he fought a battle of attrition with the 'Sun God' to devour her very soul.

"Thank God it was only a dream," they reminded each other in horror. "Though perhaps it was a warning or an Oman of sorts that the following night could offer much more than, well, 'just good fun'!" announced Maria, fearful of her life though accepting that there might be little that she or anyone else for that matter could do to protect her. "If it were true of course!" she spoke calmly.

"Too much had taken place and too many lose ends needed tying," Maria considered thoughtfully as she soaked in a steaming bath, leaving an annoyed Sonny to shout her frustrations to the closed door that confronted her, reminding Maria that she'd prepared it for herself earlier. Maria laughed, having locked the door quickly shouting, "beat you to it sister dear," leaving Sonny to stomp off in a huff, discarding a bath towel that did little to hide her modesty as she returned to her room to sulk.

Maria's concerns continued without interruption as again she considered her position within the household, though finding that her determination to leave the mill-cottage once and for all was again frustrated by that strong compulsion to remain. A compulsion seemingly way beyond her control leaving her confused mind trying desperately to understand such feelings. She couldn't!

The day was filled with fun and joy as the procession of carnival floats, marching bands, cheer leaders and a varying number of other entertainments headed towards the main congregational area conveniently situated by the 'Horse and Groom' pub and the village green. The Landlord and his wife, as a gesture of their goodwill, and to ensure that future customer service would be guaranteed a boost supplied drinks and food, after which the crowds made their way to enjoy 'all the fun of the fare'.

Yet again the sun had cleared away an early morning mist, with another warm and sunny day accredited to the 'Sun God's' determination that today of all days should receive in full its seal of approval. The Martins' family swimming pool proved an inviting option to all the revilement down the road, with Maria's intention to enjoy herself later superseded - but only for the time being - by the lure of a cooling dip and the opportunity to relax with a martini and ice.

Peter and his wife were due to arrive later, something that she was really looking forward too though with mixed reservations as she lay back in the sun-chair to soak up the sun's rays, intent on ensuring that her body would display the radiance of a 'Sun Goddess', "just for him!"

Sonny had left for the carnival with her 'builder hunk' having decided that her dark features would not serve any benefit from an extended tan, though the skimpy attire she was wearing did little to protect her from the sun or anything else for that matter. Arthur had retired to his 'den' having received a request from the 'village elders' to devise some fake medieval shackles for the initiations later. His initial reluctance had been overshadowed by the emphasis shown in ensuring that 'quick release' catches should be installed as a safety addition, something that the original binding couldn't offer and, that the whole scenario would benefit with a slightly more aesthetic appeal.

"What's the world coming too," he'd pondered for a moment, reflecting on his own initiation, with just a belly full of stout and a good woman to follow entitling him to reap all the benefits that went with belonging to 'The Grand Order of the Sun God'.

"Now, well!" He just laughed.

The arrival of Peter and Fiona was greeted with an overriding enthusiasm from his mother, and a loving hug from his father who had just returned from the 'den' after a job well done. The family had not seen them since their marriage and honeymoon in Barbados, though Fiona's lack of what might be considered as a 'respectable tan' did little to justify such an exotic holiday in the sun.

Maria offered a more cautious approach with a, "lovely to see you again darling," and, "what a beautiful dress," though thinking how ghastly such a revealing 'Chandler' style slink little number looked on a girl who might be better suited to something slightly less trendy, her jealousy of her sister in law evident within snide innuendos and cynical overtones that did little to justify what many might consider as totally unjustified. Fiona was in fact both charming and sophisticated, with a rare beauty that even Maria could find hard to match. Her figure displayed a simple charm that lacked nothing, but blended discreetly with a measurable amount of demureness that simply annoyed Maria more than anything.

"Who does she think she's kidding, there's nothing shy or modest about that one," she would grumble, determined that one day she would put her to the test.

Poor Maria tried desperately not to display her adoration of her charming, good looking giant-of an adopted-brother, though the word adopted being just a word of preference rather than choice were Peter was concerned.

"A simple word just to ensure that people didn't deduce their own conclusions if inadvertently she gave vent to her true feelings," she had decided smugly. "He was after all just a brother in the adopted sense and no more, which gave her the right to pursue his advances if she so chose. Though his marriage had induced something of an insurmountable obstacle to any attempt she might have considered on that score," she mused, less than confident that he would ever suggest that, "THEY should make love sometime!" Still, she could live in hope!

Standing to greet them she radiated sex appeal as she hugged Peter with a passion that convinced Fiona that this was something more than just sister/brotherly affection. Her eyes followed the contours of a figure that dismissed its skimpy entrapments with contempt as her breasts swelled from within the confounds of their hiding place, leaving her loins to strain at the breach in an attempt to seek freedom while offering themselves unreservedly and without mitigation to her darling Peter.

"Bloody slut", Fiona muttered angrily under her breath, though for the time being at least deciding to reserve further judgement on her interpretation of her observations as she kissed Maria on the cheek, unable to resist a note of both sarcasm and sympathy to her bikini with, "and that yellow, why it's certainly your colour, and its resilience in standing up to such demands put upon it is quite remarkable darling," she continued with a demurring smile.

Maria laughed off her remarks, inviting her to join her while Peter spent time with his parents, though remaining intent in seeing that the dear Fiona would remember the occasion of her visit with some regret.

"Oh, by the way, Sonny has a bikini that would fit you to a tee Darling," Maria insisted to an enthused Fiona with a slight smirk and a subtle hint of sarcasm, knowing that she hated the expression 'Darling' directed at herself having been used unequivocally to annoy her. And, with the added bonus in also knowing full well that Sonny was a good three sizes larger than Fiona, Maria felt that the following two hours or so could prove very entertaining.

"Come, let me show you Sonny's room, Darling!" she emphasised again, restricting her mirth at what was to take place. "Please, follow me," she motioned as she headed back to the cottage.

Fiona willingly accepted, "the sun was certainly strong and her tan could do with topping up," she announced as they went indoors. The bikini was a bright red, and its translucent fabric - although doing little to cover Sonny - offered more than ample security to an unsure Fiona as Maria watched her struggling to cover her breasts in the loosely fitting garment.

Gulping with suppressed laughter as her imagination ran riot Maria went over the possibilities that Fiona might have to endure. If she lent too far forwards the top would fall off, if she stretched too far the bottoms would slide down. She couldn't wait!

"The bikini looks fine," Maria lied, although perhaps a few extra pounds in the right quarters would have ensured 'the perfect fit'," she smiled sympathetically, beckoning Fiona to follow her.

Fiona approached the pool intent on displaying her own wears to the small group of neighbours and friends that had been invited to join them, though the Richards had declined the offer, with Mrs Richards still aggrieved at the loss of her son and lack of a conviction, and rightfully convinced in her understanding that, "without such a conviction to help her come to terms with their loss, then as far as she was concerned Sonny could well have been the killer," with the family's intent on moving from the area as soon as possible restricted only by the problems they'd encountered in trying to sell their property.

"And what about the other unsolved and horrific murders that had taken place at the mill-cottage, with nobody brought to account," Mrs Richards had shuddered, having shared her concerns with the village clergyman only the other day, leaving the poor man to offer a sympathetic ear though conveniently choosing to take a back seat in all that had taken place.

"Of course my dear, dreadful," he had agreed nervously, having considered his position as the Lord's advocate on numerous occasions and finding himself failing on all counts. His Pagan roots were just too strong!

Peter returned to the pool side, chatting to Maria their eyes following Fiona as she demonstrated her recently acquired aerobic obsession to a fascinated group of admirers, offering encouragement to all in an enthused desire that they should follow suit. Maria waited in anticipation as the bikini hovered precariously above and below its dependents, the top gradually slipping from her breasts with each enthused stretch whilst the bottoms sank gracefully to rest just below her lower abdomen. Fiona's inspired display continued to take all her concentrations, her eyes searching the heavens for some divine assistance to secure the agility required for such a versatile performance. Her modest though firmly shaped breasts moved in unison, having now escaped from their incarceration as reaching for her toes the finally rounded cheeks of her bottom expanded and contracted oblivious to the fabric's demise. In one last desperate bid to justify its existence the fabric clung to her loins, though for the unfortunate Fiona having now exposed the thick expanse of blond pubic hairs that had unjustly become entrenched within an orifice moist from the damnation such energetic infusions had bestowed on it, as glued to the spot Fiona finally failed abysmally to preserve any dignity left worthy of preservation.

"For God's sake," Maria laughed out loud, "what does your dear wife think she's playing at," she remarked to the astonished Peter, his eyes focused on a backside that he'd now become familiar with over the past few months. Now standing naked her curvaceous features offering gratuity to a smiling audience her bikini bottom slid to her ankles, having relented to the force of gravity such nakedness offering embarrassment and mirth as covering her loins with hands that offered little success she ran – or one might consider 'tripped' – her way back to the cottage in tears.

Peter continued to watch, completely dumfounded at this unwitting display of erotica, as turning to Maria with a smile he announced that, "he should go and console his poor wife, she's been under a lot of strain recently what with the farm, and now that's she's pregnant of course."

"Pregnant!" muttered Maria in horror, "you never said!"

"Sorry sweat-heart," he smiled, "but you never asked, did you!"

Maria's face fell as her eyes moistened, "what chance did she have now," she muttered, though brightening for a moment at the thought of that stupid Fiona naked by the pool. "That should teach the silly cow not to make fun of me," she laughed to herself, "and for taking my beloved Peter away from me, and now for being bloody pregnant," she muttered angrily, tears seeping from large brown eyes that had grown weary of crying. Would she ever learn?

Chapter X

Following Peter inside Maria headed for her bedroom, throwing herself languidly across the bed as she stared soulfully across at the window and on to the solitary shape of the 'Druid Stone'. Its appearance offered substance to any suggestion that tonight it would be waiting for her, and, that she must prepare herself. This hypnotic commune remained entrenched in her mind as shaking her head she closed her eyes, envisaging herself being escorted to the altar alongside her mother and Sonny her obedience unashamed as demands were put to her. "By who or what she had no idea!"

Her thoughts swirled once again in a confused disorientation, her skin tingling with a strange but pleasurable sensation as torn from reality she encouraged her dream to persist, feeling the softness of fingers blending into her skin as they soothed her tense muscles with a caressing that had her moaning and sighing. Without thought or consideration she was soon to enter into a submissive repose as those same fingers worked their way down towards loins insisting that her demands be initiated; fingers that welcomed such a suggestive appeal denying her nothing in a searching response to her proclivity. A voice whispered silently to a mind that was both receptive and absorbing.

"Tonight will be your night! Tonight will be your final opportunity to relinquish the evil within you." Reminding her that tonight she would offer herself to the 'Sun God', that she would enter into communion with her mother and sister to relinquish their souls to the 'Spirits of the Stone', and, that she should prepare both her mother and sister and herself. "She would know what to do!"

With increasing encouragement the fingers closed across the upper reaches of her abdomen, then soft and caressing as they searched successfully under her bikini top, quick to reach the hardened nipples that strained to their touch in a consuming desire not to denounce this intrusion. Straining to initiate her desires her back arched in a submissive repose, awaiting the entity to absorb itself in the pursuit of a mutual consummation as turning to her side her eyes flickered in a reflection of her passion. Her semi-consciousness conflicted with reality as sighing and moaning her arms reached out to render the mortal that was offering her so much the chance to initiate its will on her. Empty space ensued as her hands searched desperately for the body that would portray such a dream and the authenticity she so desired. It was not to be!

The spirit had left her to her imagination, an imagination that had taken her to the spirit world, where intimacy beyond her wildest dreams would be a reward she could expect and more. But not yet, not yet! Her body trembling the sweat glistening within a sheen of expectation Maria awoke to the renderings of a warbling song thrush blending with the shrill whistle of an over enthusiastic blackbird perched facetiously from the branches of a giant elm, entertaining her to a chorus of well being and good fortune as quietly she prepared herself for the evenings events feeling slightly encouraged.

Her instincts were intact her mind guided by an unseen force as she pondered on her next move. "She would deal with Sonny and her mother first! Prepare them for the initiation as instructed! She had just the thing! But first they must soak in the bath! The potion would enter the pores of their skin, to enter their mind thus rendering them obedient to her directive." It was all there, instilled in her sub-conscious, and then, only then could she deal with the remainder of her family.

They would be spared the horror and indignities awaiting both her mother and Sonny, to be excluded from the events to follow with their minds and bodies rendered both uninspired and useless. As the spirit had instructed! Nobody should get in her way! THEY would be waiting!

The family group gathered round the table for supper. It was seven-thirty, with a midsummer sun now casting dim shadows across the dinning room as if to instil a sense of urgency that soon, very soon it should command the respect it deserved. Maria, now accustomed to taking charge, emphasised the importance of readying themselves immediately after they had eaten in order not to be late for the evening's events.

"You first for the bathroom sister dear and you next mother," Maria laughed, insisting that Sonny and her mother use the bathroom first as both her and Fiona had things to discuss. "Peter and father will follow, after which Fiona and I can then prepare ourselves," retorted the enthused Maria, insisting that, "a little organisation proved necessary if they were ever going to get away in good time." She had it all worked out!

"Good thinking," applauded Peter, leaving the baffled Fiona to look on disquietly, wondering what in hell's name she could possibly discuss with that evil bitch. She was well aware that Maria had set her up with THAT bikini! "Still, it could be important," she pondered, deciding that perhaps she should wait, just to see!

Sonny did as Maria suggested, determined that Paddy would not be kept waiting although he often confused both time and dates. Maria had offered to run her bath, entering the special lotion that had mysteriously appeared in her chest of drawers earlier.

"Perhaps she should ensure that the lotion didn't harm Sonny," she worried, knowing that her actions - although acute and beyond negotiation - should still retain some concern over her well-being. Her concerns were without foundation, as the faint breeze that whispered insolvably through the leafed branches of the giant elm seemed to consolidate any fears she may have had on that score.

With Sonny now fully relaxed and having decided that Paddy deserved nothing less than a body that would evoke his senses in to capturing the full fragrance of oils she had carefully chosen, nothing would be left to chance. Unquestionably Maria's offer to brush and groom her hair and to massage - not just her shoulders - but to include her lower regions, would go a long way into seeing that a supple and therefore sexually manipulative machine would serve amply in fulfilling his demands. She was no fool!

No fool Sonny might consider herself, only this time she had proven to be fallible in such a belief as Maria carefully followed her sister's reactions as the lotion took effect. Sonny's eyes – once alert and infused with an instruction to challenge or offer a subjective repose – now stood dilated and subjective to Maria's directive as she carried out her instruction unreservedly, allowing her breasts to be fondled as sighing she rendered herself submissive to Maria's every move.

"Proof enough!" murmured a satisfied Maria. "Sonny would have denounced such an intrusion implicitly, and now she's positively revelling in it," she smiled, as rubbing her breasts thoroughly she tweaked her nipples with a smirk, instructing her to dry herself, leave the bathroom and lay on her bed dressed in just a bath towel. Maria then prepared the bath for her mother!

Amy resented any such similar suggestion to that which poor Sonny had unwittingly oozed enthusiasm too, insisting that she could brush her own hair and that her shoulders and abdominal reaches were supple enough having only yesterday been to the gym' with a relaxing massage to follow.

"And where there she had been fully attended too!" she sighed in acknowledgement to the sensuous encounter that she'd thoroughly enjoyed courtesy of a beefy young man whose willingness to succeed far outweighed his professional credentials. Amy's choice of wording immediately caused Maria to burst into laughter, as persisting she followed her mother's glazed eyes as she too became receptive to Maria's demands, with her surety in such directives proving almost identical to Sonny's, even to the point of smiling as Maria ran her fingers across her mother's receptive loins.

With Amy now completely submissive to anything that her more than persuasive daughter might have had in mind Maria felt that revenge should be sweet, having decided that her actions should be received by her mother as more than a penitence for her involvement with Tom. She now found herself unconsciously inflicting punishment by desire as her mother sighed in what might be considered as masochistic and undignified acceptance to her pleasure. Such a response was certainly enough to convince Maria that she too was now under her influence. Pulling hard at her mother's pubic hairs - just for good measure – with any persuasion into believing that her mother had unquestionably been an innocent party in that ghastly charade involving Tom's murder having always been in doubt.

"Now the time had come for her mother to face the results of her actions!" Maria decided, though still remaining fearful of what lay in store for each of them as her thoughts were directed to her own preparation.

"Very soon it would be time to ready her own body, as directed!" she frowned resolutely, though having accepted some time ago that her mortal being was now of little consequence.

Looking once again at her mother relaxing in the bath - though still remaining obedient to Maria - she instructed her to dry herself down then return to her room and rest on her bed rapped too in just a bath towel. Maria then continued down the stairs to present a fine bottle of 'Vintage 63 Chardonnay' to an enquiring father, whose concern at his wife's absence encouraged Maria to announce that, "she was resting before the festivities." Peter, as one would expect offered his encouragement to the wine and a toast ensued.

"To a great evening," he exclaimed, raising his glass as he joined his father and Fiona in consuming this nectar in one. Maria held back! Her glass remained full as she observed their eyes in anticipation. Slowly they sank to the floor, the sleeping powder ensuring that they would rest in peace for a very long time and, that their dreams would perhaps offer some consolation on having missed all the fun.

Ensuring first that each was fully unconscious she proceeded to remove their clothing, marvelling at how well endowed her dear brother was her jealousy of Fiona boiling over as she scorned at such small breasts – though far be it the case - . "And her loins…Well!" she smiled, "how on earth did they serve Peter," she scoffed, as securing their wrists and legs she looked on in satisfaction.

"If they do come too then they won't get very far," she smiled acceptingly, as dragging them ignominiously to the corner of the room and partially covering them with a tablecloth she considered her next move. For a moment she stared at them, her eyes moistening as she tried to justify her past movements.

"What she had done to her father and her dear Peter was reprehensible, but! She couldn't help herself! At least they would have no understanding that it was she who had betrayed them, and the police would no doubt conceive that a robbery had taken place. But! Did it really matter," she sighed in acceptance!

"Now to deal with Sonny and mother!" she grimaced, her heart not in it but her mind manipulated by forces way beyond her control.

Sonny was instructed to wear her white nightdress, her best one that Paddy had bought her just last week with a note inscribed, "rather rudely," she had smiled enthusiastically, as 'cum what may'! Maria helped her as her movements proved to be slow and restricted, her fascination resolute as with a touch of jealousy she observed Sonny's naked form radiating through the dim light, ready to offer itself once again to the obedience of the 'Sun God'. With a pre-arranged garland of flowers at the ready Maria placed them firmly on her sister's head. A black corded belt was then tied loosely about her waist and fastened together with a gold emblem of the sun.

"As directed!" murmured Maria unconsciously, though at the same time asking herself what in hells name was she doing as she instructed Sonny that she should wait for her next directive.

Next would be her mother! A special preparation had been devised for her! She was instructed to lay back as her pubic hairs were removed, then her hair, and then a special skull mask - the one purchased at 'Joey's Joke Shop' down in the village for their Halloween party, and the one depicting that of the Devil - was placed firmly across her head. Amy watched on in a glazed silence, her mind obedient to Maria's every move her body unflinching as with the point of a knife Maria inscribed the words 'Saturn's Salvation' in small numerical letters to her mothers lower abdomen.

The whole procedure was carried out in a methodical response to her instincts, unsure though uncaring as to its reasoning. She too was then shrouded in a white nightdress leaving Maria satisfied that the preparation had been a success with both Sonny and her mother still completely unaware of their dilemma. Having ensured that her mother remained comfortable she directed her to await further instructions. She did so impassively!

Next she must prepare herself in readiness for the big occasion; in readiness as her 'dream' had instructed to head the procession followed close to her side by Sonny and her mother. Her dress would be as Sonny's, although an inverted insignia depicting 'The Devil Goddess Esaustica' would to be placed about her neck. Then, consumed with the fragrance of incense at fifteen minutes to the hour and shortly before the sun was due to set they would make their way to the 'Druid Stone', to embrace the reverence that had been bestowed upon them as they observed the sun's dying rays penetrating the gap in the 'Stone', hitting the mill's foundations as it lost itself in the shadows.

They would await their fate at the hands of 'The Ancient Master'! A man renowned for his wisdom and expertise in the ancient arts of sorcery and witchcraft, of unknown origin and age, and, who had travelled from distant lands especially for the occasion!

The air had cooled, with little or no sound as if the world had stood still in anticipation of what was to come. For a moment Maria hesitated then, with a sigh she assisted her mother and Sonny to the door, offering them jackets as a protectorate to their modesty until their arrival at the 'Druid Stone'.

"Come, follow me," she instructed, directing them to walk submissively to her side across the field where life had been such fun with her feelings for Peter extracting every ounce of resistance as memories of those happier times flooded back. Looking at Sonny for a moment her emotions churned inconsolably within a mind demanding that hesitation or failure to endorse each and every given directive would bring the wrath of the Spirits to bare down upon her, to confound her soul and expose her weakness to the 'Sun God'. She was left with little choice as again that whisper echoed feverishly in her ear, to constantly remind her of the decree bestowed upon her and offering her no escape. On, on towards the 'Stone', mother and daughter both in Zombie like state as they stumbled through the thick bracken and gorse; on and on following Maria completely oblivious to their moves or anyone else's for that matter.

It was now almost ten thirty as the sky burnt crimson red, displaying a resplendent demonstration of the 'Sun God's' power as the giant, orange ball of flame sank little by little towards the distant horizon. Arriving as instructed Maria stood to the centre, with Sonny to her right her mother to her left their eyes levelled directly at the wizen figure standing before them.

Removing their jackets Maria then presented Sonny and Amy's bodies in surrender to the spirits. Then stepping forward she bowed to the increasingly impulsive and disconcerted little man who stood ready with a silver goblet, offering a potion - not dissimilar in content to that previously consumed at last year's festivities - to all three. With a willingness to comply they drank from the goblet at their disposal, and then quietly they were lead to the awaiting altars.

The light of a full moon sat ready in its attempt to do justice to the sun's departure, casting eerie shadows across the field, smiling almost in a sympathetic gesture of condolences on the small group who now prepared themselves for what they believed was to come next. Little did they know!

With well prepared exactness the shackles were secured, their positions adjusted in readiness for the sacrificial offerings to be subjected to their usual undignified torment as each in turn the chickens were impaled on the stakes. Only these weren't the expected half frozen chickens as first thought. No! These chickens were live! The chickens squawked in terror as the stakes sealed their fate, their throats slit as their life-blood dripped in a despondent reflection to their screeches, to be collected in a silver chalice and placed at the foot of the Stone.

The fires were lit as the flapping chickens surrendered their souls, to be sacrificed to the force that had ensured their mortality, that very same force whom now extracted pain and suffering as a means of appeasement to their being. The time had now come for the ceremony to commence as the flames from the newly enthused bonfire continued to rage, leaving the small group who'd remained to follow events watching on in enthralled silence.

Each had been handpicked from a now dispersed crowd that had seen enough, having expressed their obvious disgust with some having vague though concerted memories of last years events. In what might be conceived as a merciful act the 'Ancient Master' enforced further mouthfuls of the potion down the willing throats of the human sacrifices. They were ready!

Calling on the spirits of the dead the 'Ancient Master' instructed that those still present could remain to witness and help in the 'Millennium Initiation' as they in turn consumed large mouthfuls of the potion; a potion that would induce memory loss, thus dispelling any complicated recounts of what was to come.

Minutes past and then, the 'Druid Stone' came to light, glowing in an enthused display of colours as it transcended into the embodiment of something that was beyond description or form, infusing the atmosphere with whispery shadows that encircled its being in a magical display of antagonism to the three women before them, each transforming into that of a child as they agonised over their tortured souls their translucent beings offering some mystical enchantment that bore all the hallmarks of evil.

Each lost soul had been the victim of persecution in the village at sometime or other over the many centuries of corruption and wrongdoing, and now they were back to reap their revenge on the hapless figures that hung before them. Three mortals who would be offered as a gratuity to the stone's benevolence in offering asylum to those restless spirits seeking settlement and peace!

The 'Ancient Master' produced a long sacrificial dagger its gold handle encrusted in precious stones the thin blade reflecting the flames as they sought to devour such a splendid feast before them.

"But not yet! Not yet!" cried the Master as he sliced the garments from their persons, to expose their nakedness as their bodies convulsed in a spasmodic reaction to the drugs and heat, their minds lost in a haze of exuberance as unflinching they awaited their fate.

The spirits contorted in a frenzied reincarnation of their souls, to create a giant vortex inducing the flames of each fire to be consumed into one horrendous fireball, to offer an unremitting acknowledgement to their untimely demise within the personification of the evil they'd endured.

Sonny's glazed eyes pleaded for exoneration from these spirits, having accepted that perhaps a previous reincarnation had entrusted itself with the murder of one of these poor souls and that now it was time to pay the ultimate price as the flames shrouded her thoughts, to be lost forever her pleas for mercy either ignored or unheard. The fireball clenched its fist as it tightened its grip on the naked body it surrounded, eating deep into the flesh in an unemotional desire to squeeze the life from poor Sonny as her final screams lost themselves in an atmosphere shrouded within the putrid stench of scorched flesh.

Awaiting their fate, both Amy and Maria remained motionless, devoid of any emotion though now conscious to their thoughts. But time was not wasted in formality or trivia as the body of Amy shook violently, to contort in a grotesque devolution of her human form, to transfigure into the embodiment of some hideous Neanderthal looking creature, offering itself in an unaccepted recognition to its being as the flames induced a moment of anguish to its face. Screeching out for redemption its mortality surrendered itself to the fire as for a moment the figure of Amy reappeared, only to be swallowed up in the fireball her mortal epitaph lost for an eternity to transcend into the heavens and from there…?

Maria had willingly accepted her fate, uncompromising and without complaint. She now knew that she was the earthly embodiment of Jack Salter, the man responsible for that little girl Rosie's death all those years past. The spirits had reserved judgement on her being to last, to savour her pleas for forgiveness as the remaining onlookers followed in astonishment the 'Ancient Master's' commendation of her soul to the 'Druid Stone' and, the 'Sun God'!

Maria watched in an accepted fascination as the flames licked at her feet, resigned to her death as the numbed pain reminded her of the misery that had been inflicted on her throughout her younger life. Her eyes focused on the 'Ancient Master' for the last time, watching in reconciliatory wonderment as his body glowed in recognition of his master his face contorting into a snarl; a snarl that although communicating with the devil was not under his influence as his eyes divulged into a piercing red, dilating to consume her thoughts as her unmoving lips echoed the voice of Jack Salter.

The voice was hollow, though deep and quavering as it left the lips of a Maria now devoid of any rational thought.

"I repent my sins! I plead for your forgiveness! I acknowledge my failings! And! I pay homage to the Sun God!" [2]

For the last time Maria's unmoving lips voiced not that of an unscrupulous landowner whose merciless actions had contributed to so much misery. No! To that of a young child who had experienced horror and torment and who had tried to flee from a father whose incarnate was that of the very man that now sought forgiveness and who had insisted that she accept that his relationship with her should involve sexual understanding.

Maria's mortal being had been that of a child whose suffering had reinstated itself once again, and who would now have the opportunity to avenge herself through such suffering if she so wished. But she had chosen forgiveness, had availed herself through such suffering to allow the evil that had chosen asylum within her to transform as her father. His death had been quick, his neck broken his body ripped to shreds by a force that only now she could recognise; recognise as that of her protective spirit who had watched over her until the end. His death in a pub brawl had been a lie, a lie to wipe clean any memory she may have had of the wood, the mine shaft and the old mill where she had been sexually abused, and where her body had been subjected to a degrading list of evil demands that had inflicted both psychological as well as physical trauma and suffering.

"I remember!" she cried out loud, as the hidden memories of Jack Salter's reinstatement within a mortal framework to personify that as no less than that of her father divulged themselves cruelly to a mind tortured and cursed with obscenities. She had allowed her body to be used as a chalice, a domicile for forgiveness.

"I remember the hurt you inflicted you sadistic bastard," she wept, as the flames engulfed her personification, to render her mortal form to be burnt in a sacrificial homicide that only few would understand. But forgiveness had been offered on her terms and in an acceptance that her spirit would live on, to transcend above all mortal beings and in doing so to do as it wished. And it would!

The 'Ancient Master's' face reverted back to its unique form, its demonic eyes now restful and alert as in a voice both raised and harmonious he announced that, "this woman Amy has appeased the Devil, sacrificing her body but not her soul so that the soul of Maria and that which had been within her might rest without fear or sustenance to relinquish that which had been bestowed upon them by the 'Sun God'. Evil would prevail no longer within the Devil's immortal mantle as agreed."

Quick to acknowledge the shrouded remnants of a fun loving Sonny, who had taken life as it came and who'd asked for little in exchange he continued, "And she gave her life to immortalise those spirits that suffered at the hand of villagers throughout the centuries. Her love for life will in no way be forgotten, accrediting her spirit to future happiness within a world where her soul will be acknowledged by the 'Sun God'!"

Then, pointing to what once had been an exemplification of both beauty and youth but that now hung in grotesque disfigurement to neither, he stared for a moment as if almost accepting that perhaps Maria of all people should have continued in epitomizing such charms to a world where so much misery and ugliness reigned throughout. Continuing in a voice both soft and faltering, with an underlying demand that this was a statement that should not be ignored he made reference to Jack Salter.

"Now, finally, his soul and hers can rest in peace, to be immortalised in a celestial forgiveness alongside the sacrificial statements of both her sister Sonny and her dear mother Amy. Both were innocent victims not only to His greed, his merciless countenance and murderous gratuity, but to that of those who both preceded and continued to follow in his shadow, with their unmerciful intolerance to their victims showing neither repentance nor attrition. Due to the shame brought upon this village by such callous brutality to its children these three women before you have been ostracised from their mortality, finally to meet their death that through death they should be immortalised!"

"Praise and obedience to the 'Sun God'!" he cried soulfully, as bowing his head he paid homage to the 'Druid Stone'.

The once gentle breeze that had lent itself as a cooling agent to a night both balmy and discourteous now increased within a cyclonic definite in a swirl of unimaginable versatility. Within an instance the once personified remains of Sonny,

Amy and Maria were swept from their incarceration as the Druid stone awaited their arrival, accepting them within its asylum to be commemorated alongside a spiritual covenant demanded by the 'Sun God'.

As if accepting that their moment in time had come the sirens of police cars broke the silence of the night, their eerie dialogue to the horrors yet to confront them conforming in an acknowledged understanding that this was a problem to be understood and dealt with within the confounds of a crime that would prove to be unsolvable.

Both confused and scared the small group of shocked onlookers quickly dispersed into the night, to wined their way home having accepted that what they had just witnessed was nothing less than a God given characterisation of something that had to be; something that the ancients had decreed was above all the laws governing modern day society, with no questions asked or sought to signify anything else. They would remember little!

Detective Chief Inspector Jacob Conrad walked slowly towards the 'Ancient Master', leaving several of his local officers pacing calmly in the distance unconcerned. Jacob Conrad had conceded that the necessity for Pagan ritual must continue whatever as a few words were exchanged within a mutual understanding of harmony and respect. Returning to his men he instructed them to leave. They had witnessed nothing, with the Inspector having received assurance that the area had been cleansed and returned to the spirits within the stone, with no trace of the night's events left to offer further investigation, just memories of a beautiful girl alongside that of her sister and mother, whose bodies would never be found and whose deaths had been witnessed by nobody, except!

Revving engines signified the departure of the police the undoubted necessary investigations put on hold with the Inspector having decided that to precede with such would have been pointless. Until the morning that was! The 'Sun God' demanded his continuing allegiance!

About the Author:

Graham W Harwood was born and bred in Liverpool, and after a somewhat rock-n-roll stay in boarding school he intentionally got himself expelled at the age of just sixteen to join the Royal Marines. This in effect was like 'jumping out of the frying pan into the fire'!

Having experienced many a happy time during his early childhood holidaying in Devon - and now finding himself stationed in Devon - he came to love the county, thus the reason why his present novel and three of his still unpublished stories reflect this image.

Whilst serving abroad in Borneo he was badly injured, leaving him paralysed from the chest down and confined to a wheelchair. Having moved to Eastbourne as the years past his flair for writing both poetry and short stories developed, until only quite recently he decided to take what he had always considered as 'just a pass-time' a little more seriously. Self taught and in effect still an amateur 'The House That Jack Built' was written without thought or consideration to its contents. He just wrote!

Text from story:

At first Maria walked slowly, finding it difficult to see in the increasing mist as picking up speed she stumbled on a flagstone causing the strap on her shoe to loosen.

"Damn!" she acknowledged, stopping under a streetlamp as she stooped to adjust the offending item, her concentration disturbed by the sound of heavy breathing to her rear. Her sense of foreboding increased as each menacing and disconcerting breath infused an overpowering acknowledgement of fearful apprehension and acceptance to her vulnerability. She froze!

Slowly she turned, her eyes focusing in horror as a hand reached out menacingly from the shadows. She went to scream, but her mouth was dry as her whispered vocal chords croaked out a desperate plea for, "mercy!" As without thinking her fingers automatically grasped firmly about the handle of a bag that stood ready to fend off whatever this monster had in store for her.

The hand stretched cautiously towards her shoulder, the breathing increased, louder, consuming and almost screaming at her within a crescendo of decibels. Her body tingled, goose-pimpled and cold as trembling in fear and trepidation she could feel the weight as the fingers clamped firmly about the damp flesh covering a body that had almost resigned itself to the inevitable.

An arm followed, gruesome, like an entwining tentacle ready to squeeze the last ounce of oxygen from lungs that felt ready to burst as she held her breath.

Then a shoulder! Broad and menacing, demonic in its entirety and ready to smother her in an embrace of certain death!

And then a face! A face that offered a broad and concerned smile and that wished her no harm. It was the face of her brother Peter; dear Peter who had been sent to search for her by her worried parents. Such was her imagination!

Printed in the United Kingdom
by Lightning Source UK Ltd.
131147UK00001B/1-54/P